Searching for the G Spot

by Peller Marion

Artemis Arts Library
San Francisco
2004

Searching for the G Spot

Artemis Arts Library USA
San Francisco, CA 94111
www.Artemisartslibrary.com

First Edition

Printed in the United States of America

Designed by Laurence Brauer, Wordsworth

ISBN 0-9746927-6-X

Dedicated to my husband, Ron

1

"Tantric what?"

"Tantric sex," she said very softly, keeping her eyes on the narrow mountain road.

"It's Tantric sex!" he shouted in disbelief. "This weekend workshop is about sex?"

His voice echoed in the enclosed cab of the spanking new white convertible she had rented at the airport. She had insisted on a car with low miles. Despite the humidity and the unrelenting heat, Ralph demanded that she keep the top up and the air conditioning on high.

"You brought me to Tortola for this?"

He sat low in his seat with his shoulders hunched up, still wearing his parka from the plane ride. She could see the neckline of his "He who dies with the most toys wins" sweatshirt. She had stripped at the airport rest room and changed into a flowered cotton dress with spaghetti straps.

"I thought this would be a great vacation gift to us." She took one hand off the wheel and patted him on the knee, carefully keeping the car from going over the centerline on the wide two-lane highway. Her stomach was unsettled and brewing with irritability from the long flight, despite the ocean and sky rising expansively like soft pastel flannel ahead of them.

"If you don't like it, we don't have to stay." Paula knew she was bluffing as she heard herself forming her words quickly, the way she did when she felt caught.

"What are they going to teach me, that I don't already know?"

"Oh, probably nothing."

Just like a guy, she thought, but she didn't want to tamper with his mood. She knew that he could dig in his heels, like a truculent little boy, if she pushed too hard, so she kept silent.

She gave the car a little more gas, pressing hard into the soles of her Arche sandals, and glanced at her Gucci watch. She had bought these just for the trip. Shopping was a spiritual experience, and she loved to spend her money. It was a refuge when her life became too overwhelming from the demands of her work. If they didn't get lost, they could still make it to the lodge in time for dinner.

Slowly the road grew narrow and the terrain began changing into dense and shrouded green kudzu-like foliage. It clung to fences, draped over trees and created organic caves with dark openings; then it crept along the ground meeting the shoulder of the road.

The radio blared Robert Palmer's song, "Addicted To Love," but Paula was puzzled about love as they drove further away from the airport. On her right, a yellow road sign with a bold squiggly line showed ten miles of hairpin turns ahead. She wasn't turning back now. They were almost there.

Ralph leaned against the car door and fingered the controls of the air conditioning until he had to shout over the burr of blasting cold air. She changed the station to a news report about the Reagan administration's new budget spending, then back again to "Addicted To Love." The repetitive chorus and Ralph's fidgeting made her edgy, and she pushed his hand away from the knobs on the console. With a single quick movement, she switched off the radio. "You're such a control freak," he bellowed.

An argument was brewing, and she knew that she would have to take the offensive to win. She had gotten them this far, and she felt spiky, self-righteous and ready to take him on. She may have been petite and the youngest child in her family, but she made up for it with her quick tongue and temper.

She just couldn't follow her own advice about keeping quiet any longer. She took his bait.

"C'mon, look who's talking." Her voice filled the confined space as the humidity mixed with the new smell of cold engine air and created a kind of clamminess.

"You have to be kidding," he countered. "I'm so sick and tired of you trying to manipulate me."

He suddenly leaned forward in his seat. She glanced over at him quickly and then put her eyes back on the winding road. "You'll make me have an accident!"

"Do you actually know where we are going?" He felt spiteful now.

"Yes. I'm not *manipulating* you." She elongated her words for the effect. "Other husbands would kill for a surprise like this. What's wrong with surprising you?"

He turned to face her for the first time. The late afternoon sun cast flat shadows on his angular jaw. "You've surprised me a little *too* often for your own good. I'm still recovering from when you painted the wall of our bedroom fuchsia, or enrolled us in a four thousand dollar tango class without telling me."

She could feel when she was in real trouble with him, because his soft blue eyes turned a blue-gray color, like a stormy sea. Now they were becoming hard and opaque — the beginning signs.

"Hell, I couldn't tango alone! Oh, come on — the tango was different. Besides, you told me later that you thought fuchsia softened our bedroom at night, and aren't you glad that you *can* tango now while all the other husbands look on with envy?"

She shot him a disgusted look and wished that he would just get off it. Other husbands seemed so compliant — at least from a distance.

"I had hoped I could lie on the beach, eat some good meals, snorkel and catch up on my sleep," Ralph said.

He had been working very hard, and she knew that. They both had high-powered careers.

"Yeah, your idea of a vacation is to barricade yourself in a sterile hotel room with a big-screen television, a bathroom the size of a gym with a hot body-pounding shower, a gargantuan bed and twenty-four hour room service. How nourishing to the soul is that?"

She stopped to breathe. She was gaining momentum now, but he jumped in.

"You just can't appreciate that can you? Your idea of a vacation is staying in some Beatrix Potter rabbit warren of a bed and breakfast and oh-ing and ah-ing over the wife's bric-a-brac."

She was thinking of a time they vacationed in Weaverville and stayed at a place strangely named The Victorian Inn, but there was nothing Victorian about it. It was the owner's idea of a space age hotel with red painted walls and black Naugahyde upholstered furniture that looked like the vacation spa of the Marquis De Sade. But hey, Ralph had loved it.

"Remember The Dream Inn," Ralph countered, "and the first night we stayed in that 'discombobularium.' I slept on the floor because the room was the size of a birdcage and I could bounce from the tiny bed and out the door. The owners dressed up to look like my grandma and grandpa even though they were younger then us. The bathroom was so small that I could barely turn around to pee. You got us a room that was a converted closet for two hundred dollars a night!"

Paula had loved the place. It was a little brown shingle cottage with roses and wisteria covering the front door.

"I'm really a *big* fan of converted closets! You don't take into consideration that I'm a big guy and I need space! Then we had to make conversation with these creeps still in costume as our grandparents the next morning at breakfast. Oh, you forget those things, don't you?"

"It was so cute the way they served us soft-boiled eggs in the porcelain egg cups with hand-painted flowers on them."

"Spare me!"

"Weaverville was your idea anyway! You didn't want to spend any money on a real vacation like this one."

They had argued themselves into a silence. The ocean whizzed by on the right. Cars passed them and some drivers waved. You could always tell tourists from the locals by the white rental Avis Mustang convertibles.

"If I don't like this workshop, I'm going on my own vacation."

Paula glued her anger-filled eyes to the road and was silent. A pang of fear gripped her stomach as she thought of this possibility. Their ten-year marriage remained a mystery to her. How was it that people looked like they were doing so well and then one day a friend would tell her that the Quinces or the Adamses were filing for a divorce? The whole ugly story would spill out like sludge, and it had been there all along. Had these couples made a pact not to tell anyone, or did they not know it themselves until it was ready to become undone? Who was it that said families are miserable, but they are miserable in their own way?

Why was it that moments like Weaverville were memories that gave her insight into the man she had married, but worse, they became those defining moments in a marriage, when she recognized and had to admit to herself how different their tastes were. The romantic stage was definitely over.

She wondered about the real mystery of coupling. Maybe the seeds of growth and the seeds of destruction both were virulent in the soil of marriage, and like weeds and flowers in a garden, daily they were duking it out.

"Why did you sign us up for this?" he asked.

"Isn't it self-explanatory? A tautology?"

"A what?"

"Never mind!"

"Sex equals intimacy, closeness, better sex equals a better marriage?"

Snookie, her best friend, said that people do grow apart; they lose interest. Why judge them, when nothing in life is permanent anyway? Isn't that what the great teachers said, Jesus and Buddha? She never heard of Mrs. Jesus or Mrs. Buddha.

Her mind drifted back to her visit with Dr. Jacobs, a new gynecologist Snookie McGants had referred her to. Snookie suggested that Paula had better have an exam before she embarked on this journey involving the lower regions of her body.

Snookie would know. She was an expert on sex and truth in relationships between men and women. She had written more than ten books on the subject and had been divorced eight times. She told skeptics in her audience early on, "I'm a veteran in what not to do. You have the good fortune to learn from my mistakes. That's why I counsel people on it." Her most recent book, *Couples for Keeps,* launched her onto the bestseller list *and* the *Oprah Winfrey Show.* Paula was filled with admiration.

The crashing surf was on her left, and down below she could see wind surfers skimming the waves. On her right were steep red clay banks covered with blue flowering ice plants. Life here certainly looked just like her picture of paradise.

Although Tantric Sex was the rage in Marin quite awhile ago, it took Paula all this time to work up her courage and give it a try. As her thoughts turned to her friend Snookie and to her visit to Dr. Jacobs' office, her life partner Ralph fell into a deep silence, thinking about how he could slip out of her plans and get to his own "personal space."

2

If Snookie could get absorbed in anyone outside herself, it was clearly a small miracle. How could you say that of a bona fide psychologist and someone who helps people with their problems? Yet, if her clients' problems didn't in some way reflect on Snookie's good taste, her knowledge and good looks, she was not interested. Her magnetism, which she worked on like a Hollywood starlet, caused an endless stream of men young and old to sit at her feet. Sex was her claim and recognition was her game.

Snookie, with her red-haired mane, was called "Hot Pants McGants" in the early seventies because she was thin, leggy, came from a rich Episcopalian family and wore hot pants on campus. Next to Snookie, Paula often felt like the 'before' picture. She was so happy that she had found Snookie, and had often wished that she had found her sooner than graduate school.

This morning was no exception to vintage Snookie. Once a week Snookie McGants had a half-hour program about relationships on Marin's KNEX radio, and singles all over Marin were talking about her latest research findings.

Unlike the cultural wisdom that the length of a man's penis could be determined by his nose or shoe size, Snookie reported on a recent Canadian study performed with two thousand men between the ages of thirty-five and fifty. Researchers found that the size and shape of a man's kneecap was the determining factor of the adult size of a penis.

She got extensive television coverage when she showed that a flat round kneecap was indicative of a rather short penis, whereas a bulbous and longitudinal cap indicated a somewhat prominent and large penis that could extend considerably.

She couldn't wait to discuss her excitement with Paula at finding yet another thing to keep her face in the news.

"Can you imagine what this does for the dating game?" Snookie explained to Paula after the show, as they sipped coffee at the Hot Spot Café in Mill Valley. It was a place where psychotherapists, real estate agents, health nuts, and wannabe writers sat two feet away in every direction. One had only to wonder out loud about a personal dilemma, and four or five people would present their services.

"Do you think you may find women peering under tables in restaurants and finding excuses to lift men's trouser legs?" Paula asked

They were so bonded because they had shared a few life-threatening experiences that they treasured like precious stones. Snookie was whip smart and an interpersonal wizard if you didn't count her marriages and lapses in judgment.

"No, no, you don't understand. As a scientist, I have publicized a rather remote but well-researched study that will leave my mark on humankind. In turn, women will thank me for this one obvious indicator. I mean bringing it out in the open. No pun intended."

"I am truly happy for you," Paula said, unmoved, and then she let out a little sigh. She was trying to recall whether she had ever taken notice of Ralph's kneecaps in their long years of conjugal servitude. She made a mental note that she must go home and check him out.

Besides, she was busy observing the details, the bodily minutiae, Snookie's clothing particulars. She was getting so caught up in her beauty mark, like Claudia Shiffer's, her cute ears, the missing top button of her silk blouse, that she was lagging behind the men in the café in organizing Snookie's individual features into an overall impression. It was only now that she was watching a craggy elderly jogger smiling wolfishly at Snookie, from the corner of the restaurant, that the fact of Snookie's beauty occurred to her. Why was it that women got caught up in the details of other women? Ralph said that most women dressed for other women. Snookie dressed for men.

Snookie leaned forward and whispered loudly above the din of the espresso coffee machine, but Paula was no longer listening.

"Everyone has at least one tragic flaw," Paula explained to Ralph when she first met him. "Snookie's is falling for the same-type jock who doubles as a con man and bilks her out of her hard-earned savings. To Snookie's credit, she saves one couple and their marriage at a time, just not her own. Snookie is the Mother Theresa of easy rescues for couples." Ralph had liked her immediately. What was there not to like? Snookie and Paula had both been girl scouts in school and cheerleaders in their respective high schools.

Snookie and Paula had the camaraderie and zeal of professional athletes in how they confided in each other. They knew every detail of the other's life from the day they met to the present, including the type of vibrator each owned or discarded over the years.

Snookie glanced out the window at the red brick Mill Valley Town Square, up at the framed photographs on the wall of local celebrities, and then focused on Paula.

"I believe, with this news coverage, that I could start a pre-owned and certified clearinghouse for men," Snookie said. Then she bounced to her feet and did a calf stretch. Paula gave out an audible sigh and propped her head in her palm.

Paula had never seen another girlfriend interrupt an intimate conversation to exercise, jogging in place, doing deep knee bends or leg lunges.

"I sit all day listening to people, and my tush gets numb. So I've got to stand and talk, or stretch and talk when my meter isn't running," Snookie had told her long ago. So that now, when Snookie popped up and jogged in place in the middle of a dinner conversation, Paula and Ralph just took it for granted, along with her other misdemeanors like belching. Paula and Ralph tried to practice the California thing of being non-judgmental.

"How would you do this new enterprise? Aren't you already the champion in that arena, I mean in your own personal dating situation?" Paula asked.

She was thinking how for most people, honesty was such an unusual departure from their standard modus operandi. It was such an irregularity in their workaday outpourings that they felt obliged to alert you when a moment of sincerity was coming on. "To be completely honest," they would say, or, "To tell you the truth" or "Can I be straight?" Often they would want to extract vows of discretion from you before going any further. "This is strictly between us, right . . .? You must promise not to tell anyone. . . ." Snookie didn't do any of that. She tossed out intimate and unflattering truths about herself and others all the time, without a second thought.

"I've got to belch. Wait. Okay." She stopped and moved away from the table and then moved back to continue. "This is God's honest secret. Can I be straight with you without telling anyone?"

"Snookie, for God's sake we've known each other. . . ." Paula was startled to learn after all these years of friendship that Snookie too had boundaries of discretion.

"Okay. Okay. Well, You know how BMWs have these pre-owned cars that are certified? Well, wouldn't divorced women want to have a clearinghouse to come to or call and get the dirty low-down on men over fifty that they might want to date?"

"Yeah, and come to think of it most men have been 'pre-owned' by their ex-wives, and you are in exactly the right profession to make it successful! I mean you have the gene pool."

They fell into gales of laughter.

"You'd be doing a great service to womankind," continued Paula, as she sipped her non-fat, decaffeinated, macchiato, mocha soymilk latte.

She leaned closer and whispered, "Snookie, seriously? Do all marriages get like this?"

"Like what?"

The noise in the café seemed to diminish and Paula put her palm to the side of her mouth, lowered her voice and whispered dramatically, "Never mind!"

Then she stopped, and waved Snookie away. She didn't want to say anything more to Snookie. On some level that would be admitting defeat and painting a picture of herself as not having it together. Coupling was one area of their friendship where Paula seemed to excel, while Snookie racked up husband after husband. Snookie just couldn't seem to break the code.

"No really, honey, what is it?"

"I can't. It is too hard." Paula's eyes got moist and a tear formed in the corner. It began rolling down her cheek, taking with it her layer of Lancôme Sports Tint Cover Up.

Snookie fumbled around for a tissue in her oversized purse and then grabbed a napkin that came with her three-ounce paper cup filled with a shot of spirulina. She handed it over.

Paula kept shaking her head and wiping her eyes. Although Paula felt she could say literally anything to Snookie, it was difficult to spill these beans. Even this disclosure was hard and painful. It was so hard to get it out, even to her blood buddy, without appearing like a big failure.

"Tell me!" Snookie insisted.

Paula sniffled, wiped her eyes, looked straight at Snookie and bit the bullet.

"It's Ralph. I want a divorce!" She paused. She felt as though she had just admitted that she murdered her mother.

They both sat there silent and stunned, absorbing the thought.

Then Paula added as an afterthought, "He doesn't know anything about this, so don't say a word."

"Oh no! Oh no!"

Snookie shook her head, as if she couldn't accept this thought. She sat silently pondering, while bicyclists in their sneakers with clip-on cleats and spandex outfits made tapping noises walking to their tables with Styrofoam cups of steaming coffee.

"But you've been together so long!"

Snookie and Paula both guessed that they could burn out everyone with their intensity and energy, given half a chance. They never really talked about it, though. Ralph was the only one who had stuck around. Paula had been in all kinds of therapy on and off for years with many psychologists and psychiatrists. Secretly she knew that she was a therapy junkie. She had long ago admitted it to herself that she needed a paid friend.

"But why?" asked Snookie.

"It's beginning to feel like my mom and dad's marriage. They act like one person. My mom finishes my dad's sentences."

"So Ralph is getting on your nerves? Is that it?"

Paula let out a big sigh. Snookie reached for her hand in concern.

"He's just so boring!"

"I know you better than you think! There is more going on here! Reframe it! Change your mind! Honey, any woman on the verge of menopause is high maintenance. You just can't trust your body or your emotions any more. Doesn't Ralph know that? Isn't he sympathetic, helpful?"

Paula nibbled listlessly on their shared order of a low-fat Spirulina scone.

She slid the plate in front of Snookie to taste. Instead, Snookie pushed it aside, still holding on to Paula's hand across the table. Snookie couldn't bear to see her friend so unhappy.

"Look, I know that this marriage thing can be quite a bitch. But you need a perspective here. I love you and Ralph. You both are so good together. I remember how you told me that within five minutes of meeting him you thought you could *marry* this man. How big was that! You guys laugh a lot, and that really helps a marriage. Besides, he has a real job!"

With that, Snookie and Paula leaned back and laughed at Snookie's self-effacing joke. And then Snookie let out a small belch.

"No, it's everything these days: my work, my libido is waning. It feels like things that I could multi-task several years ago, do with my eyes closed, now take so much more time. I get so stressed-out and tired."

"What does Ralph feel?"

"When I am too stressed to have sex, Ralph takes it personally. He is worried about his signs of aging. He is hitting fifty-five and he constantly worries about his health. He's certain he's going to die of a long protracted disease and waste away alone. Some mornings I just look into his face and know what the rest of the day will be like for me."

"Is that true? Any *real* health problems?"

"Well, actually he has everything that he reads about, sees on television or someone else has." She tried to be light and humorous about this. But she knew it was true.

"How do you feel about that?"

"No, I'm just joking, but he is my second biggest source of stress outside of my job, my television ratings and trying to sell my new coffee table book. If I got on *Oprah* with it, it would really raise the ratings of our show. Of course, this is my first book, not like your successes."

"That's a lot of stress, sweetheart. What's the title?"

"The title is, *Whatever Happened to Gidget? A Dictionary of People Not On the Hollywood Walk of Fame.*"

"You mean they weren't famous enough?"

"Not only that, they disappeared from sight, like people on our show."

Snookie knew better than to ask more questions, because she thought that Paula didn't have a snowball's chance in hell of getting published, much less going on a publicity tour. Paula seemed delusional about this, but Snookie wasn't going to burst her bubble. After all, what were good friends for, anyway?

"Let's talk about your successes," Paula said. "Your problems seem more interesting than mine. Besides, I'm not exactly the compassionate type towards Ralph's complaints. I feel more like Nurse Ratchet in *One Flew Over the Cuckoo's Nest*. That puts somewhat of a damper on our sex life. Yes, especially now that he thinks he is losing his edge, I mean age-wise in his field. I don't know if it's really true."

Paula was thinking how paranoid he was. He thought that management was plotting to fire him as creative director of his advertising firm. In fact, she caught him looking through one of those electronic catalogues to see if he could find some device to bug his workplace.

"Men never surrender to the inevitability of aging," Paula said. "You know how men are: I-can-handle-it-myself. Besides, he is a tightwad when it comes to spending money. If, God forbid, he needed heart surgery, he'd try to operate on himself."

"Do you two have quality time as a couple? Many couples who have been together a long time have pictures of how they want to change one another. Maybe if you spend some time away, in a new setting perhaps, you can see each other in a new light."

"Yeah, we are lucky we don't have kids."

"Relaxation can prolong his life, you know. That's the secret key to health and longevity." Snookie paused and took a small dainty bite out of the scone that she had ignored up until now. "I am just trying to be helpful, because I see the pain you're in, honey."

They both took a moment to stare out the picture window at the commanding view of Mt. Tamalpais from inside the café. All the bicyclists were amassing outside on the square, gearing up for their weekly ride to Stinson Beach. Paula noted how well Snookie was aging despite the fact that she was three years older than her.

"Maybe Ralph has been working too hard and you both need a break. It'll give you a chance to see other facets of him again in a relaxed setting."

Paula grinned at the idea of relaxing with Ralph. "He can be very funny. Every now and then, he has uncontrollable urges to 'share'. Give him some caffeine and he will reminisce for hours on the most romantic times in our relationship. Did you know he has the ability to recognize faces from the past in a crowd? He's always telling me what it was like growing up in Hollywood and going to Hollywood High School. He prides himself on recognizing Hollywood stars, when he goes home for a visit. Once we saw an old woman with liver spots shuttling by with her walker in Trader

Joe's. He went right up to her and spoke to her. Turns out she was Myrna Loy, the 'thirties actress."

That's a skill I should have, she thought. It is so wasted on him. Paula frowned. "But sometimes he is so unresponsive. So I say, 'stomp once if the answer is yes, and stomp twice if the answer is no, big fella.' That's why I've recently thought of divorce, if not murder."

Snookie shook her head. "Divorce won't solve your problems. Remember that you take yourself wherever you go."

"Can you love someone, but just not stand them? He does strange things, like the time he hired the one-armed cleaning lady. He said, 'I thought she would be cheaper and I was helping her out.'"

Snookie smiled. She loved how entertaining her friend could be even in times of trouble.

"How about Hamid, the Iranian travel agent he engaged? Hamid was just learning his geography of the United States. Ralph wanted to fly to Newark. Hamid booked him a flight that landed in Philadelphia. When Ralph confronted him about his error, Hamid said, 'Oh, on a map of the States it was only a quarter of an inch away.' Ralph wasn't even angry like I would have been. He just rented a car and backtracked three hours to Newark."

"Maybe you married him because he has a generous heart."

"But forever?" Paula leaned forward with an air of confidentiality. Her face was animated with expression. "Sometimes I find myself thinking of ways to kill him. These feelings surprise me. Is this normal?"

"How frequently do you feel this way?"

"It's unexpected, like when I'm shopping at Whole Foods, or jogging down Tennessee Valley Road. Something just seizes my mind. It lasts several minutes. I've watched *Unsolved Mysteries* and *Ten Most Wanted* and read too many news stories about how a paid hit person can botch up the job. I'd have to do it myself to get it right. I argue with myself: should it be slow and systematic or fast and sudden?"

"Oh, honey."

"Did you see the movie *Black Widow,* or *Fatal Attraction*? Ralph calls it a husband training film. I could put rat poison in his coffee, and he would die slowly. Recently I put a half of an anti-depressant into a vase of cut flowers when I couldn't find an aspirin."

"An aspirin?"

"Yes, that's supposed to keep the flowers fresh. The flowers froze into the strangest bloom and stayed that way for a solid month. I often wonder what small systematic doses of these types of medications would do on husbands?"

"Paula! I am shocked."

"I would hire the best lawyers, and claim an unprecedented defense like in the Dan White Case, the Twinkie defense. Remember, he was the guy who killed the San Francisco mayor. His defense argument was that he was hypoglycemic. Too much sugar in his system, a bad diet, caused him to distort reality and gun the mayor down. I could use the Menopause Defense. It's hot flashes and night sweats."

Snookie shifted in her chair and said, "Murder will solve nothing. You're joking, your problems would run much deeper then."

Paula was on a roll now that she had a listener. "Women from all over the country would rally around me, shave their heads, protest and march on Washington on my behalf. I would be an icon, a menopause poster girl. People would finally take this phenomenon seriously."

"Paula, the worst thing you can do is act out! You must know by now that actions like this have consequences. You must get ahold of your imagination. There is no magic cure."

They both identified with the Me Generation. She guessed that made for some pretty self-absorbed people. Like Ralph, who worried a lot and stayed awake half the night. He blamed his illnesses on something mysterious.

"Terminally Unique, eh?" Then Snookie said thoughtfully, "You need a vacation in the tropics somewhere to de-stress and focus on your relationship with Ralph again. I know *exactly* the workshop that will heal all that stresses you, and before you go, a trip to Dr. Jacobs is needed."

"Snookie, what I don't need is yet another therapist. With all the money I've spent on therapists, I've made them rich. I must have bought them their down payments on their mansions, their yachts and all the Jaguars you've seen zooming around Marin over the last decade."

"I wish I had you for a client!" laughed Snookie.

The crowd of brightly clad cyclists had thinned out of the café. A Mexican man was left clattering dirty dishes from the tables to the kitchen, and the counter girl, in her teens with several body piercings in unlikely places, was making a new pot of coffee for the lunch crowd. Paula heard the sound of water filling the large urn.

"Dr. Jacobs is a gynecologist. He's *special! He* could help you figure out this menopause thing, or I'm not Snookie McGants!" With that she slipped her hand into her purse and came out with Dr. Jacobs' card and handed it to Paula. "Here is your magic pill."

3

Dr. Jacobs had a reputation as one of the best-liked gynecologists in Marin County. He was still slender. He was careful about his weight, and he walked to work with a light and vigorous step that marked him as physically fit for a man in his mid-fifties. He favored expensive alligator shoes.

In fact, he looked a bit like a reptile himself, with a shiny leathery pate and some thinning hair. He thought well enough of himself to decorate his scalp by brushing a few strands of remaining brown hair across it.

His deeply set eyes were reminiscent of the intensity of Yasir Arafat. And in the mornings, his whites were red from insomnia or perhaps a baby delivery that came during the wee hours. But this sleep disorder did not distract much from a charming quality of stubborn youthfulness.

His only flaws were a slight speech impediment that made him flick his tongue and lick his lips intermittently when he talked, and the fact that he was lonely. This was well hidden behind his professional demeanor. In medical school, he was called "The Tongue," while most of the other interns were considered "Breast Men." This only seemed to add to his unusual charm.

His square jaw enhanced a sensitivity of face that expressed genuine interest in each woman. Women patients, who were all he solicited by the very nature of his practice, commented that it seemed like time stood still when they were with him.

On the morning of Paula's first appointment, she noticed that his waiting room was done up by a local interior decorator in various tones of clay color. Pictures of babies he had delivered cuddled by their ecstatic moms lined the walls, and women were knee-deep, patiently waiting for him. Built-in seats, upholstered in an earthy shade of mocha, lined the four walls of the room. Women in various stages of pregnancy filled the seats. While they listened to ethereal New Age instrumentals, it occurred to Paula that there were no windows in the waiting area. How thoughtful, she reflected, that it was designed intentionally to give the feeling of a gigantic womb.

On the stroke of ten, a small woman wearing a housecoat with little bunnies printed on it, waddled portentously towards her. Her white plastic name tag read: Serena, Nurse Practitioner.

"Dr. Jacobs always likes to be on time, unlike other doctors in the county. He likes to give you all the time you need," she said to no one in particular. She extended her hand, smiled and ushered Paula into a room.

Inside the examining room, Paula looked around. She saw no photographs in elaborate frames of a wife or children. Serena noticed her scanning the room. "You'll find that he has a wonderful bedside manner," she said as if to make up for the omission of the obligatory family pictures. She wrapped a rubber blood pressure cuff around Paula's arm and pulled it tight, saying, "This won't hurt." Then she sighed. "This your first time here?"

Paula nodded. "Snookie McGants referred me."

"Oh, Dr. McGants. I've read all her books. She's brilliant. She paused and then added, "but you will find The Doctor brilliant, too. I just love working here."

Paula smiled politely.

"Because I just love working for him. Women say that he's a cross between Deepak Chopra and Billy Graham." Serena pumped up the rubber blood pressure bulb. "Women flock to him. They've told me that they have more intimacy with him in fifteen minutes than in twenty years of marriage with their husbands." She noted Paula's blood pressure data on a clipboard, and then handed her a green cotton gown. Snookie had told her that Dr. Jacobs was no male chauvinist pig. Local lore had it that those types of men had been chased out of Marin years ago.

Serena smiled. "The opening is in the front. You know, for the breast exam and pap smear."

"I can never get these things on right." Paula fumbled with the gown. Serena helped her tie the strings just as Dr. Jacobs slipped quietly into the examining room, smiled at Paula, and nodded to Serena, who finished quickly and closed the door quietly behind her.

After the initial introductions, Dr. Jacobs studied Paula carefully. She was an attractive woman in her mid-fifties — probably in the throes of menopause. He noticed the wiry ends of her colored oxidized brown hair. It was in a short stylish cut that definitely spelled a professional woman, he thought.

Dr. Jacobs noted that she had drying skin, and wrinkles were appearing vertically on her well-mapped face, which caused her to look tired and older than her age. He knew from past experience that when a woman's wrinkles started appearing in this manner, she was well on her way to a waning libido. This immediately activated "The Tongue's" rescue fantasies.

He ceremoniously repositioned his glasses on his face and asked, "Is this an annual visit or is there something specific I can help you with?"

"Just an annual visit."

"How is your health in general?"

"Good."

Dr. Jacobs gently ducked under the white cotton cover that housed Paula's body, but he continued to carry on the conversation, from this headless perspective, as if he were sitting in her living room drinking a martini. That's how comfortable he made her feel.

"I've warmed this up for you," he said gently as he inserted the speculum into Paula.

She took a deep breath. These kinds of visits made her usually feel tentative and afraid, but somehow with him she wasn't hesitant at all.

Dr. Jacobs thought of himself as a coal miner going down into the tunnel of love, but this tunnel was fleshy and pink. With his headband tight around his forehead, that housed a small but penetrating halogen light, the tools of his trade, he readjusted Paula's feet into the pre-warmed flannel stirrups. Paula noticed that the flannel had the same bunny print as the nurse practitioner's housecoat.

"Are you going through a new life stage?" Dr. Jacobs asked.

Spread out before him were the never-ending mysteries of female pulchritude: ten centimeters long and five centimeters wide. This was his domain.

He could see the answer before him in the fading pinkish-gray walls of her vagina, but he had learned to talk in metaphors. Thereby he would not be offensive.

"Do you mean menopause?"

"Yes."

"I haven't actually gone *through* menopause, but I'm approaching it," Paula admitted, "very rapidly, in fact."

"Let me get a few slides here. This will only take a minute."

She heard his muffled voice under the white cotton cave and felt some quick twitches from the speculum, she supposed, and cool air rushing into her open cavity.

Dr. Jacob's head popped out from under the white cover.

"I always like to find out as much as I can about my patients. It helps with my understanding of them." He smiled. "For example, do you work?"

"I'm the producer of *Almost Making It!*."

"Making it?"

"That Los Angeles-based television program about people who were famous and then slipped from sight. Well, we catch up with them and find out what they have been doing with their lives since."

"So you're in entertainment. That must be glamorous work."

"Yes, it is very exciting."

If he only knew, Paula thought. She didn't find it all that exciting to be in pursuit of the losers in Hollywood. It's not like she tried to find real movie stars who have disappeared. She had producers who did all the work to find real second-stringers. Trying to find people who bombed out on television and movies just to produce a show about it was often nerve-racking.

She secretly called it the Recognition Recovery Program. Ex-stars were still legends in their own minds despite how low they had fallen. That's after she tracked them down in drug rehab or homeless shelters and interviewed them with her crew. Diligently she tried to piece together the hopeful part of their sorry, sad lives after they self-destructed. She had just written a book entitled *Almost Making It!*. At this very moment, her agent was trying to get it sold by shopping it around. Her career was dependent on the publishing and sales of this book. The executives in her business were very fickle if ratings went down, even for a moment.

Dr. Jacobs' face came out of the covers again. He smiled and flicked his tongue. "Now this will feel really wet, but I must get this slide." Then he ducked back in.

Paula suddenly felt warm and open in her lower parts. She was getting wetter, like she felt from foreplay with Ralph. She had never experienced anything like that before in a gynecologist's office.

"Do you do a lot of traveling?" he asked from under the cover.

"Well, yes. You know tours, radio shows, *Oprah*."

His face appeared. "You've been on *Oprah*?"

God, she reflected, Snookie is right. *This guy is an incredible doctor. I'm definitely feeling something!*

"What are you doing that feels so good?" asked Paula.

"Oh, I'm just testing your vaginal reflexes," Dr. Jacobs said very seriously as he continued to chat.

Under her section of the white cave of cotton, Paula was relaxing into wonderful sensations that were the product of Dr. Jacobs' testing. She was getting wetter and more relaxed.

She wanted to stop talking and just enjoy the ecstasy that Dr. Jacobs was producing, but she tried to be polite and behave like a patient should. After all, she couldn't very well tell him that she was about to climax, because maybe he didn't know what he was doing. Everyone's body responds differently.

He repeated his question as he dodged back under the cotton tunnel. "Have you been on *Oprah*?"

Paula was trying to think of the next thing to say, when suddenly she felt soft pink waves of warmth that were undulating deep inside her and streaming down her legs.

"OOOOOhhhhhaaaprah," groaned Paula, writhing on the table.

Dr. Jacobs tried to quell his unabashed excitement. His lips were moist as if he had been gorging on a juicy ripe mango, and his eyes were wet. His head popped up from under the cover, he wiped his mouth, and he looked tenderly at Paula. A more in-tune person could have seen small beads of sweat that had recently formed beneath his thinning pate.

"Well, I think we've gotten what we've come for," he said gently. "You can rise slowly now. Here, let me help you."

When Paula was making love with Ralph, she couldn't stop thinking about the calls she had to make. Often, Ralph felt to her like a fast-moving freight train coming into the station. This was a new sensation that she could grow to enjoy.

He lifted her slowly from the table. Paula wasn't steady on her feet. He helped her to her clothes. "Get into your clothes and the nurse will come in and show you into my inner office."

Paula wondered if she felt what she thought she felt. It all had happened so suddenly. It was like the time she jogged past a nude flasher one early morning on Storrow Drive in Cambridge. *Did this just happen?* she wondered in disbelief.

Dr. Jacobs had a beatific smile on his face as he left the room. He had never had a patient who had really been on *Oprah*, although he had had several who had hallucinated about Oprah and their own guest appearance.

Once Paula was inside Dr. Jacobs' inner office, he leaned forward with renewed interest. They chatted away like old lovers after a sexual encounter. "So you are the person who produces that show about people who just missed stardom and their chance to succeed? Interesting."

"Yes."

"I bet there are some people who would kill to have your job," Dr. Jacobs said wistfully.

Paula nodded.

"How does your husband feel about having a celebrity in the family?"

"He's okay with it." Ralph actually seemed indifferent to or jealous about it at times. "In fact, that's how I met my husband. I was sitting next to him on my commute flight from Los Angeles to San Francisco when the plane suddenly dropped in altitude. We took one look at each other and hung on for dear life. He really saved my life. I was hysterical when we finally recovered. He had to calm me down, and that's how we began our relationship."

Meeting Ralph, after so many abortive relationships, was the closest she had ever come to magic. It wasn't his appearance alone that drew her to him, but he had something inside that shone through him. It was a certain depth of spirit that she saw in, and she knew that he'd be important in her life.

"Besides," Paula continued, "I'm not exactly a celebrity."

"I mean, how does Ralph feel about your traveling, does he join you?"

Gawd, she thought, how awful would that be, trapped in a sterile hotel room night after night with Ralph?

"No, he is coping. You know that marital relationships can get routine, after all." *He's coping my ass, Paula reflected. If only he weren't so . . . so. . . .*

"How long have you been married? Ten years?" Dr. Jacobs answered his own question.

"Yeah."

Paula was having a hard time coping with the aftermath of what she was feeling in the lower half of her body and the need to use her head at the same time.

"We're doing fine."

Dr. Jacobs suddenly stood up.

"Well, we are done." Dr. Jacobs smiled at her. His lips were wet and his eyes were moist. "You know, everything looks pretty good with you from this end. I'll have the results to you in the next week or so, but only if the pap smear is negative."

"You'd be happy to know that we *are* going to a workshop in Tortola, British Virgin Islands, on Tantric sex."

Dr. Jacob's jaw dropped. He turned pale. "That's great, really great," he said abruptly.

Paula sensed that the rapport she had with him had vanished, and she didn't know why.

"And who are the leaders?" he asked in a new formal tone.

"Sky Spacious and Yogianni, do you know their work?"

"Er , no." Dr. Jacobs' voice took on a tone of forced evenness. He shifted in his seat and looked at his fingernails.

She wondered if she had said something wrong.

Dr. Jacobs looked at her seriously. Surely over the years clients like her, with their health insurance, had afforded him many purchases: a forty-seven-foot yacht, a five thousand-square foot home in Belvedere, and a new twenty-five foot swimming pool. After the enjoyable time together, he was wondering if it wasn't time to give something back, despite his displeasure with what he heard.

"Our time is up, and it has been a pleasure meeting you." He gave her a knowing look. "But before you go, let me prescribe an anti-depressant. I have some samples here. This may help you get through this phase of your journey. It helps with moods."

He handed her a blue packet no larger than the size of a best-selling paperback. "Take one a day as indicated, they are time-release. I think these will be of benefit to you. Vacation is a good time to begin these."

Her confusion about Dr. Jacobs' response to her telling him about the sex workshop blew out of her mind and only the good parts of the encounter remained.

And that's how Paula walked out of Dr. Jacobs's office that afternoon with a thirty-day supply of Wellbutrin, a six-month supply of Astroglide, an E-string, birth control pills and dozens of little individual samples of KY Vaginal Moisturizer. She dug into the shopping bag he had given her with all her new supplies. She looked at each little blue pill of Wellbutrin, sparkling in the sunlight in its individually wrapped plastic casing. Each had its name written on its face. The letters formed a happy face smile on the front of the pill in small purple letters. The smile matched Paula's.

4

Silently, Paula congratulated herself as the taxi sped to the airport. She felt like a thief pulling off a grand heist, one where you drug the victim, throw him in a sack, hoist him into the trunk of the car and then speed away. She had planned and paid for the trip all on-line. In addition, she was getting two continuing education credits at Marin State for it.

Two drinks later and thirty-seven thousand miles above the earth's surface, Ralph was doing fine, even a bit elated. His long legs in his size fifteen Nike sneakers splayed open, blocking the aisle. His broad-shouldered six-foot-five body looked like it had been stuffed into his seat. To strangers sitting across the aisle, he appeared like a decompressing workaholic with high alcohol content. Yet, in a way, he and Paula could also be mistaken for a sweet middle-aged couple on an early morning flight out of San Francisco airport. They both had that wearied-from-work look on their faces.

Except for the time Ralph won a raffle for a free overnight at Lake Tahoe, they hadn't taken a vacation in all their years of marriage. She remembered how they had to sit through a three-hour sales presentation on buying a time-share in order to get the prize.

He always had an excuse. "What about the cost?" he complained.

"It's our vacation," she retorted. She knew it was a lame excuse, but vacation spending didn't count in Paula's mind.

At home, they spent less and less time together. They saw each other at the beginning and end of the day. Maybe that's why God invented work, Paula mused, so people can go off to places and make other people, strangers, miserable.

She ripped open the Velcro of her platform sandals and freed her feet. The salt from the honey-roasted peanuts she had eaten was expanding into her rapidly swelling ankles. She was becoming a Petri dish of sodium and water.

Assessing the situation as her husband slept, she saw his skin was pasty and he was looking gaunt. He definitely needed some sun. His snores made little spurts and gurgles, as if he were swimming under water. That's when she remembered that she had forgotten to bring her snorkel equipment and wondered if he had remembered his. He was more forgetful than she, so it wasn't likely, she mused, as she looked at his head full of silver hair. So many men she knew were balding, balding or bald. Men really do change with age, she reflected. Their faces seem to get smaller and their noses and ears bigger with age. Ralph said there were two kinds of bald: the matte head and the shiny head. Matte was better because it didn't reflect the light the way shiny did, calling attention to one's aging. Even with Ralph's full head of hair, he was very concerned about what the future held in store regarding his hairline. "Thinning" was the term he used. Each morning he stood in front of the mirror and asked her if she noticed any thinning.

As the plane took off, it lurched to the right. Immediately, Paula began praying. She had created her own do-it-yourself religion in fourth grade when she won a gigantic cellophane-wrapped popcorn bunny in a raffle by repeating the same prayer day and night for a week: "Dear God, let me win the popcorn bunny." This episode had forever cemented her own personal relationship with God.

Once airborne, the voice of a woman pilot came on the loud speaker. "My name is Vera Potensky, I am your pilot for this trip. We are flying at an altitude of thirty-seven thousand feet. A hurricane was forecasted to hit the island by nightfall. Fortunately, it has been downgraded to a tropical storm. Luckily we've gotten clearance to take off, because at first we weren't sure. You might feel some turbulence though. So please keep your seat belts on."

The plane kept lurching and then leveling out. "Oh God, a woman pilot!" Ralph moaned loudly.

He leaned into Paula. "And she has a Polish name! Do you think she is *competent* enough to fly us there?"

Paula sank down in her seat and swallowed some Rescue Remedy, caught the attendant's eye and ordered two vodkas. She drank each directly from the tiny bottles.

During the flight, Ralph developed one of his many illness symptoms, a coughing-sniffing spell, which caused several passengers to put down their magazines and stare, perhaps contemplating a seat change. His face turned beet-red and his nose ran. His hair, originally perfectly groomed, now resembled Clarabell the Clown from rubbing against the back of the seat.

"I think I am catching a cold from the recycled air!" he said and popped up in search of the flight attendant. The passengers went back to their reading. All during the flight, Paula couldn't get comfortable herself. The air in the cabin was intermittently stuffy; stifling hot or gusting recycled smelly wind. The cabin smelled of a combination of leftover food, wet socks, and expelled gas from people sitting too long.

As the plane descended, Ralph was nowhere to be found, even when the "Fasten seat belts" sign went on.

Paula began to panic so she hoisted herself out of her seat to see if he was in back talking to someone. Ralph was gone. When the flight attendants took their seats and buckled up, Paula really got worried.

"Where is he? Why isn't he back in his seat?" she muttered.

Then suddenly, she knew. A bathroom was situated on either side of the two seated and buckled-in attendants. As the plane descended, one door was flapping wildly open and shut.

Ralph must be seated on the toilet, his pants down around his ankles, trying to reach out with his hand to close and lock the door. Couldn't he reach?

Oh, God, should I help him? Should I alert the flight attendants? she thought.

Maybe he is reacting badly to the flight after all, and getting even by disappearing. Her women's group, which Ralph fondly called The Men Trashers, had said that their spouses sometimes had this reaction from too much nagging, but Ralph had never done it before. Ralph had even gone so far as to say that her women's group should buy pastel silk bomber jackets that had *Men Trashers* embroidered on the back.

Paula felt sick to her stomach with anxiety, trying to go over in her mind again and again where Ralph could be on the plane. It only sat two hundred and fifty with four attendants and nowhere to hide. It *must* be the bathroom. How embarrassing for him.

When the plane finally landed and was taxiing to the terminal, Paula was able to get the attention of an attendant. At that precise moment, Ralph came walking out of the cockpit, smiling and chatting with the woman pilot.

"You'd never believe what Vera told me," he said to Paula. "She graduated from Hollywood High just like me."

So began their first real vacation in paradise.

5

Antonio poured another cup of coffee into his favorite over-sized plastic mug. He was drawn to it at the Recycle Circus because it was made out of two heat-resistant walls of plastic with colorful confetti swimming between the two layers. As an afterthought, he added a shot of brandy to the drink. He was excited and hopeful as he glanced at the wall clock. It was only ten in the morning and a long humid day stretched before him. He lived alone outside of town and was as self-contained as a baked potato.

He was waiting for the sound of the doorbell and hoping that the latest ad in the *Tortola Times* was witty enough to bring a new crop of seasoned and spontaneous tropical honeys right to his doorstep outside of Smuggler's Cove. Sky told him that because he worked on the property, he could get into the Tantric sex workshop free if he brought a companion.

"The Gods Don't Exert," had always been his private motto. A smile came over his face, and then he uttered a short snort, amusing himself at this thought. He may have used the line when he was young and virile, but at seventy he still had a big sexual appetite. A short, compact man who gave off an intense sexual vibe, he wasn't sure whether all his equipment still worked. Maybe this workshop would give him a seventy-thousand-mile tune-up.

At night, while trying to get to sleep, he tried to reconnoiter back in his mind his last real sexual encounter. It seemed longer ago than he cared to remember, or perhaps even his memory was failing him.

Could it have been so long ago? He tried to connect events and milestones to the act, as if the act itself was but part of a larger dance. Was it with his lovely assistant who volunteered to be on his Yoga tapes? She had been enthralled with the fact that he had put Hatha Yoga on the map with his book which made the bestseller list nationwide. His book was all the rage in the 'sixties, and so were his tapes. Now what remained were remainders in cartons in his back garage. On the cover of each tape and book was his close-up headshot that strongly resembled his guru, Yogi Whas Sup Gee. Antonio had looked young and virile at that time, and his books still remained a good hustling gimmick. He had given one to every new prospect. He hoped that each young lady would recognize the Yogi Whas Sup Gee resemblance. During that time in his life, he had been mistaken for his guru in airports and movie lines, and he loved that. Was that so very long ago? How about all the flirtations and near misses on the beach? That was a very good site for nude sunbathing, and he made a mental note to go there soon again. He reflected that people over fifty-five should wear laminated pictures hung around their necks of what they looked like when they were younger, like they do at high school reunions. That way they could show their best assets.

However, his appetite for excitement had landed him in jail. As a kid, he hung out with blacks. White kids at Cleveland Jefferson High used to tease him about his hair. "Brillo Head" was his nickname.

Later he moved to Los Angeles and became a record mogul for Columbia. He discovered Martha and The Soup Stones in a back yard of a tenement singing for their supper. He found Shardella in a juke joint and pulled her up to stardom. He changed her name and her look, and gave her some glitz. He was one of those men who seemed to over-admire women, so that his adoration appeared ingenuous.

That was after he was sent to Folsom for check kiting thirty-five years ago. Now he was working at the Retreat Center as gatekeeper. No one could possibly imagine from this little man's demeanor how big his star had shone at one time.

He adjusted his Tommy Bahama wide-collared shirt, fingered the eighteen-carat gold chains around his neck, and ran his hand through his full head of curly graying hair. He was thinking about his latest coup in the *Tortola Times*. The personal ad read: "Middle-aged gentleman from Madrid with energy-a-go-go looking for lactose-intolerant Goddess. Let's make beautiful music together." He got a lot of mileage out of this Spanish thing, although he really came from the ghettos of New York.

Suddenly, he heard a high, familiar ring, so he sauntered over to the screen door. Outside stood a woman about fifty, backlit by the sun. A pleasant sensation registered in Antonio's brain.

He congratulated himself. His technique always amazed him. Spread a wide net and reel in the fish. He smiled and snorted softly at his good luck.

"Hi, I'm Chakra Sante."

The stranger put her hand up to her brow and peered through the screen into the darkness of the hallway. Antonio opened the screen door and ushered her in.

"Oh, what a lovely home you have."

"I hope you had no trouble finding it," Antonio said politely. "Come into the kitchen and I'll make us a cool drink."

He glanced purposefully as she pulled her belly in, pushed her chest out, and swayed past him into the back of the house. He admired her curly shoulder-length platinum hair and hoop earrings. She wore a skirt made of diaphanous material, very complicated, with lots of floating layers, and a see-through peasant blouse that housed more than adequate breasts. He could see that he would enjoy pleasuring her.

Chakra giggled and whirled around. "I guess I should tell you that I didn't come alone. I brought my girlfriend Moon Dancer with me. She's a belly dancer and a tarot reader. Would you like your future read?"

"Oh, two for the price of one?"

Antonio and Chakra laughed together. She brushed his arm with her fingers.

He hesitated and then said, "Sure, where is she?"

Chakra held up one finger to indicate that she'd be right back and ran down the hallway and out, leaving the screen door banging.

What Antonio saw next delighted him. It was an embarrassment of riches. The long muggy day had turned into a celebration, Tortola style. Chakra and Moon Dancer came back giggling and handed him some wildflowers that grew in his front yard, a quart of Ben and Jerry's chocolate ice cream, and three tightly rolled joints.

He ushered them into his dark cool cottage. He lowered the bamboo blinds and poured them each a tumbler full of California chardonnay in his confetti plastic mugs. "To the miracle of the printed word!" He lifted his glass. The women followed suit.

Antonio had an audience and that's all he needed to enjoy his day. That afternoon the three of them learned about each other while they shared the ice cream and became lactose intolerant. They smoked, kissed and rolled around on his Marrakech carpets. They laughingly fed each other ice cream, trying to find each other's mouths in the blue haze of cannabis.

As the sun traversed across the blue sky, in the dark cool living room of his cottage, they found themselves stoned to the bone as the three explored their new friendship. They became instant and inseparable allies, and Antonio told them how he first came to Tortola.

"I was working in a music shop in Oakland when I was a teen, and I had a fight with my live-in girlfriend, so I went back to work and decided to spend the night there. I was going to show her."

"Why did you do that?" Chakra asked, taking another toke and passing the joint to Moon Dancer.

"She said that I was messing around with other women."

"Were you?"

"Let's just say that I had a lot of juice. I was angry and wanted just to make her sweat. I slept in an empty piano box at work until about two o'clock in the morning. Then the owner's wife came in with some young black guy."

"What was she doing?"

"She started making love, slobbering all over him about two yards from my box. They were drunk. I thought it would be a quickie, but hours went by and she was still coming. You know, doing that oh-ing and ah-ing thing. I had never heard anyone come so long in my life."

"Well, maybe it just felt that way, because you were stuck inside a box," Chakra said, finishing the joint. She reached across the table and attacked the top layer of chocolate ice cream with a plastic tablespoon. It broke off in her hand.

"I tried to be quiet, but by then I had to pee awful bad."

The women doubled up with laughter.

"I was waiting for the wife to talk about me: Antonio is a great worker, or Antonio is useless. You know how it is when you are an employee. But she didn't. She was about boing-ing this guy. Finally, about six o'clock in the morning they finished and left."

"So she didn't say you were useless?" The women exchanged smiles.

"Nope, but as they left, the wife said, 'damn that Antonio, he forgot to turn on the burglar alarm.' Then she turns on the damn thing."

"Oh, boy," the women groaned.

"I finally crept out of the box and relieved myself. Then the alarm went off, and the cops came. They wanted to know what I was doing there."

The women were leaning forward on the floor, suspended in anticipation.

"I thought fast, and told the cops that I had forgotten to turn on the alarm when I left work, so I came back, and tried to get in to turn it on. Whew, I got by the skin of my teeth."

In due time, Antonio told them about the workshop at Sky's place in several days, and his availability to attend because he worked there. They couldn't wait to be escorted.

"He is so entertaining," Chakra whispered to Moon Dancer.

He didn't tell them that he would get in free if he accompanied them, because the workshop was short on women. In the morning he would call Sky and then share the news with Reefdancer, his close male friend.

Late that night after the two women had left, he felt grateful that he didn't succumb to his baser instincts, because if *it* hadn't worked, they might have decided not to go to the workshop with him. No woman wants a project to work on for the weekend.

Antonio stared at his nude body in front of the full-length bathroom mirror. His eyes fell down between his legs to his individual size-serving of salvation.

"Oh God," he muttered. "Please make it work after all this time."

6

You could not really say that Duke or Delila were fortune hunters, but for Delila the shimmer of coins and the smell of money had a particular draw. Duke, on the other hand, might reasonably have been called a common name dropper or adventure seeker.

Delila was constantly on the threshold of arriving. She was a spinner, always in motion, going one hundred and fifty miles per hour in hot pursuit of something. There always seemed to be something ready to take fire in her life.

Gold was her favorite color. She had an enviable mass of gold-blonde hair, unlike the dry seaweed-like coif of other women in their early fifties, and skin not damaged by years of tanning. No bathing suit lines. She was an expert, an aficionada, not a novice of the sun. She had learned from seasoned tanners. Let's face it: She also had good genes.

She loved gold filigree chains and flashy outfits, and knew flashier was better. She always wore red. Miracle, her best friend, had agreed that red was her "dramatic" color. (They had their colors "done" together). Delila knew she could never be rich enough or have enough gold and red on her person.

People would comment about her whitest teeth. They were all hers, not damaged by coffee or cigarettes. You could see that there, under the aging, maybe twenty-five years ago, was a foxy lady who was now forty pounds over the limit.

"I told him you were a sexy lady. A real party gal." Miracle was trying to get Delila to visit her in Tortola, and this late-night long distance phone conversation was the best way to entice Delila and abate Miracle's loneliness.

Delila might fall for the bait because she was always looking for gatherings, comparing herself to other women at all of them: their dress, their shoes, how well they were aging.

"You just seem to have it all together, and I need your help in man-hunting," Miracle said.

Delila was in a time in her life when things were not what they seemed. Miracle imagined that Delila had worked out a formula for men, diet and holding wrinkles at bay. They had met when Miracle was married to her ex-husband, the plumber. Yet, Delila's formula had stopped working and had become a slippery slope.

"You just don't know," Delila said. She was thinking about all her regrets and the time left. She acted as if this season was the last blush on the rose before a fatal bug disease snatched up the bloom.

"But you are so much the life of the party." Miracle chatted on.

Despite Delila's positive attributes, she was becoming dissipated and flaccid. She still liked to think of the life she was living as an appetizer to some wonderful entrée that would soon be served up to her. But she was finding this hope more and more difficult to sustain.

"Miracle, for the first time in my life, I feel cranky all the time. Maybe it's the change of life. Men seem to be the major offenders lately. I look at others' lives and they all look better than mine."

She didn't tell Miracle that her solitary drinking was not a buffer against her suffering and disappointment in people.

"The last time we double-dated, you flirted mercilessly. You wore that red with bare shoulders. It was fabulous." Miracle was trying to make her feel better. The dress was cut to show the separate fleshy mounds of her breasts so that when Delila leaned over they almost looked like they would flop out. She kept losing them and flirting and losing them seemed part of the flirtation.

"What I mean is that I really admired the forethought you put into your attire that evening."

Delila just wanted to feel better about herself and be *somebody*. That night neither realized that Delila would have what she wanted sooner than they thought.

Duke was a tireless man on the verge of fifty. He had an evangelical dedication to work. Maybe he was one of those men who drew all their anxiety into physical activity rather than figuring things out with his brain. Or maybe he was just plain lacking in complex cognitive functioning. But both of them never seemed touched by the monotony of saving and accumulating money for any long-term goal.

As a teenager Duke spent hours behind the barn outside of Boise, Idaho, looking through old *Playboy* and *Hustler* magazines that he copped from his dad. Spiky strapped women's heels, black sheer stockings, garter belts, and size D-cup women's breasts transfixed him, enough so that later in life, he could ejaculate by just a wave of a garter belt lightly across his chest, or the graze of a stocking on his torso. He once told his guy friend that he could kill the man who invented panty hose because they denied the access that nylon stockings and garter belts gave men.

It was no wonder then, that after three failed marriages, he fell head over heels in love with a potential number four. She fit all his imprinted criteria. She was his dream girl. His dream girl had no apparent demands.

Duke appeared to be the man to fix all of a woman's needs, with his big rough hands, red ruddy face, and take-charge personality. He had fixed a leaky faucet, climbed on the roof to burn out pesky hornets' nests, rescued lost skiers stranded high on a mountain top, and kayaked to save stranded tourists. He had large shoulders and a full head of blonde hair that made him look half his age.

Neither of his best friends, Reefdancer and Antonio, knew that he was an innocent when it came to women's manipulations and sex. They did know that he was attracted only to blonde-haired women, like his dad's girlfriend. He was wary of women bearing sexual favors.

When Duke met Delila, she was flying high. She had a great wardrobe, she had just gotten a breast augmentation, and she was living comfortably for the time being off a little trust fund her grandmother had set up. Her mother, a New York intellectual, felt that since Delila had changed her name (from Dorothy) and dropped out of Yale to follow Bagavonda Gee to India, she needed money. So her mother prevailed on her rich Chicago mother, whose descendents had come over on the Mayflower, to start a trust fund for her granddaughter.

Unlike her two older brothers who had found their way in the world, Delila was still searching. One brother was a furniture sales representative and the other, deemed the success in the family, was a high-ranking officer in an esoteric international spiritual movement.

Truth be told, Delila's family had all but given up hope for her. In fact, they couldn't hide their critical evaluation of her choices of men and career, if traipsing after a guru was a career. They didn't value the fact that Delila was a consummate learner.

Delila wanted her own unique life. And that's why on this day she was a thousand miles away from ground zero, the family compound on the East Coast. She wanted to be rich, famous, well-spoken on her own steam and an expert on something. If she couldn't be, she wanted a husband who was, so she could grab onto his coattails and go for his ride.

She was the ultimate adult-in-training, always learning about anything new in the spiritual, art, music or poetry worlds. She fretted over the spotlights shining too brightly on her, but once she was the center of attention, she basked in their raw heat.

On this particular morning, she was the center of attention because she had been invited by Pastor Estella to address the audience on the topic of "Color Therapy and Your Wardrobe." The service and her talk were held at the Unity Church in Marin.

Duke didn't know that this would be his lucky day. He had slept over at his ex-wife Joanie's house because he didn't want to go back to his lonely apartment. After languishing at her kitchen table, she invited him to this Sunday morning gathering. Duke was seated in the audience when he spied Delila literally flowing up the aisle in gold chains and an unstructured Eileen Fisher long gauzy dress: her Goddess clothes.

She dazzled the audience with her smile. He knew that he had to meet her. All these years of imprinting he had done, all those preparatory years, mapped perfectly onto this woman.

What about his ex-wife at his side? His embattled mind was grappling with the same question. Indeed, that was why she was his ex, he reassured himself.

After the service was over, and less than a nanosecond after his former wife excused herself to the ladies room,

Duke made a beeline over to Delila and used one of his sure-fire, never-fail lines.

Never one for hype or bogus one-liners, he simply planted himself squarely in front of her and said, "I couldn't leave here without meeting you. You really knock me out. Your smile reminds me of Suzanne Somers, the movie star."

"You mean the Thigh Master Queen?"

They both laughed as Duke gazed upon her beautifully formed breasts. Like many surgically augmented women who hadn't fully integrated their new experiment, she wore them like two blow-up toys suspended in front of her to be enjoyed and shown off. Truth be told, she enjoyed the expression on men's faces when they spied her new attachments.

If you had stopped Duke right then and queried him, he would have told you that he had just arrived at the doors of Nirvana.

Delila, too, halted dead in her tracks, looked him straight in the eyes and changed gears. There was something in his presentation, his broad shoulders and deep blue eyes that required her immediate attention. She tried to focus.

It was then that she felt golden warmth in her solar plexus. She flashed him one of her "I'm-the-workshop-leader-and-totally-in-control-here" smiles and handed him one of her cards. She couldn't deal with this right now, but she knew she wanted it for later.

Delila told Miracle on a long distance call that very night, "I really fell into a big one. He has millions, a big restaurateur from Steamboat."

"You've already found that out, and you just met him this morning? You are really something." Miracle chuckled at her friend's forwardness.

Later that day, Duke told his ex-wife, "She's a *real* workshop leader." Joanie, his ex, just yawned with her mouth closed.

One of the many reasons for their relational demise was Duke's inability to separate fact from fiction. He had been swept away in the moment one too many times. As a friend now and not a wife, Joanie felt it was easier to take his foibles in stride.

On a brilliantly sunny day, exactly three weeks after meeting each other, and with perfect calm, Duke and Delila packed all their belongings onto a container ship. They stood on the pier and watched their gravity boots, cross-country skis, cartons of vitamins and mineral supplements, all their worldly goods leave the Port of Oakland (Delila had ten wardrobe boxes alone, filled with her gauzy flowing goddess clothes). Then they hopped on the next flight to Tortola to live their dreams together.

The first night they arrived, they stayed at the most expensive hotel in town. After an expensive dinner, Delila fell asleep.

Duke awoke at three o'clock in the morning in Delila's arms. Lightly he extricated himself and walked out to the beach. It was that time of morning when subtle changes occurred with the tide. Like a breath, it inhaled, halted and then exhaled. Then the tide began to return, signaling the dawn. The peculiar excitement of being so far away from home, with a new wonderful woman and a whole new beginning ahead of him was more than he could contain within himself. He began to jog on the beach into the waiting sunrise.

He thought of all the other women he could be with, and the ones he could have married, the worshipful El Salvadorian house maid, the little blonde waitress from Boise, the diffident dark-skinned Latina dancer from Mexico City. (All his desires lay outside this hotel.) He looked up at the façade of the building. He imagined that he could see through the verandas into the half-opened glass doors where plastic Casablanca-fans spun at full speed. In their beds lay hundreds of sleeping couples, with warm air brushing across their skin. It occurred to him that all those strangers had dreams for themselves, too.

He was on a rock, miles away from the action, the real action. Suddenly, he felt extremely claustrophobic. If this whole reality was just another movie set, he couldn't find the way out. He started to hyperventilate and began experiencing emotional vertigo. It was like a premonition that he simply couldn't handle.

Duke went over the summary in his head: within three hours of the meeting they had slept together, within three weeks they had moved to Tortola, their dream place. Duke didn't let the fact that they were burning through Duke's nest egg and Delila's small trust fund get in the way of their fantasy life together.

Then Duke woke up one morning three months and three days later to face one immediate cold, not very hard fact: He was becoming impotent in direct proportion to the slow seepage of his net worth.

Delila had an entirely different coping style. She began each morning by sitting yoga style propped up against pillows and the headboard in their bed. She insisted that she guide them through visualizations beginning with, "And now I want you to see gold color in your solar plexus." She was certain Duke's impotence was just a rocky phase they were going through.

During the next several months, they seemed to be standing on the threshold of plenty. There were many profitable but elusive schemes they tried to sell their friends. They truly believed that by putting down ten thousand dollars in a multi-level marketing deal they could net one hundred thousand in ninety days.

They expected that everything would turn out fine. Despite their years of knocking around separately in the big impersonal world, Delila and Duke finally had found each other. They felt they were truly soul mates. They felt rewarded and blessed.

Delila, as she was prone to do, tuned into his angst in the nick of time, under the drone of ceiling fans as the humidity lay on like heavy cream. She announced, "We're going to the Tantric sex workshop tomorrow. It's time to do something wonderful together, to forget about this problem of money and sex! We've got to get you out of this funk and have some fun together!"

7

"It's so balmy and the rain is so warm here," noticed Ralph.

Paula felt bloated with honey-roasted peanuts, pretzels, and the seafood dinner that tasted as if it had been doused in paraldehyde. She just couldn't help eating on flights. They seemed embossed on her mind as food-free zones. In fact, anything in sight was fair game to stave off boredom and the uncomfortable closeness of strangers.

She drove the last few miles with the scrap of paper with the directions perched on the steering wheel. They turned at the thirty-six mile marker down a dirt road onto the grounds of the workshop.

The gatekeeper, a gray-haired man in his late sixties, introduced himself as Antonio. He led them to their small, brown-shingled cabin in a semicircle of a dozen cabins. Each had its own garden. A large separate building in the middle was the main dining area and the clubhouse.

"Once you clean up, you might want to get something to eat at the dining hall," Antonio said.

"How long have you been here?" asked Ralph.

"Oh, once I got out of Folsom, I decided that I wanted to give something back, and then I ran into Sky and Yogianni. They will be leading our workshop. I've been around for awhile, just doing handyman-type stuff." He opened the cabin door and gestured them in.

"Can I have my key?"

"We don't have keys, it's easier that way. In any case, there aren't any locks. It demonstrates our principle of openness." Antonio helped them put their bags inside the door and left.

Ralph gave Paula a wide-eyed look of disbelief.

"Let's just stay open, honey," Paula said reassuringly and kissed him on the cheek.

Inside the small room, a double bed was suspended from the middle of the ceiling by ropes and pulleys. A chair with a straw seat was the only other piece of furniture. They opened their suitcases on the floor, and Ralph headed into the bathroom. He rummaged through his toiletries and took out his organic green roll-on mosquito repellent. He rubbed it all over his arms and neck. Although he hadn't seen any mosquitoes yet, he was wary. He put several droppers full of Echinacea from a bottle wrapped in a plastic baggie into a glass half filled with water. It turned a murky brown. Quickly he gulped this down. Instinctively he knew that this was major bug territory, and he was certain that he was going to come down with some incurable disease. He took off his tee shirt and jockey shorts and stretched out on the bed before supper, mummy style, inert and taking up most of the space.

Paula busied herself by meticulously dividing the hangers in the shallow closet, putting six on the left of the hollow-core sliding door and an equal number on the right. Then she hung up the things she had brought to wear.

An hour later, after they showered and changed, they walked to the dining hall.

"What's that sound?" Ralph asked. He could hear a tiny whine in the air, like a soft, steady sound of a mosquito. He slapped his neck.

Paula grabbed his arms and pulled him through the lodge doors just in time to avoid a scene.

They took a tray and pushed it down the counter. A woman gave them a dish wrapped in aluminum foil.

"Here's your Vegan meal," she said. "We were about to close the kitchen, I'm glad you made it in time. We kept it warm for you."

They took it, almost ill with hunger.

"Listen Paula, did you sign us up for vegetarian meals while we're here?"

"Yes, I thought we both could stand to lose some weight." Paula said, realizing for the first time since the trip began that maybe she was taking on too much self-improvement at one time.

"Oh, God." He looked at the dried-out steamed rice and wilted spinach and broccoli. He led them to a table where they squeezed in alongside the other participants, sitting picnic style on two long benches. Ralph recognized Antonio seated with two women. Instead of maintaining the awkward silence, Ralph gave up on the food and turned to Antonio.

"Are you taking the workshop with us?"

"Yes, I want to learn about this stuff."

"Is that your wife?" Ralph indicated, nodding his head toward the woman seated next to Antonio.

"No, I met her recently, but she wanted to find her G spot too. I also brought another partner." Antonio touched the arm of the woman with spiky platinum hair and gravity-defying breasts shaped like miniature basketballs. She gave Ralph a toothy smile, wrapped her arm through Antonio's, indicating ownership, and continued talking to the woman next to her.

Paula caught a piece of the spiky haired woman's conversation over the din of noise. "After I woke up, I decided to get into my sexuality,"

"Woke up?" Paula scratched her head in bewilderment.

"Before I woke up, I was a housewife. Then I met Deiter Tolley-Polley Das, and I woke up to the spiritual life."

Paula wondered if she was awake or asleep. This was very confusing.

"You mean you were asleep before you met your guru? I mean he is your guru, right?"

"Yes, he is. We're all asleep until we meet our guru who wakes us up!"

This sounds like *Sleeping Beauty*, thought Paula. She felt a slight bit inadequate that no one like that had popped into her life to guide her or Ralph. Not that Ralph would ever follow anyone, not even his shadow, if he could help it.

"When you are not with your guru, what do you do with your time?"

"I'm a massage therapist, what do you do?"

"I'm a producer of *Almost Making It!*."

"Ohmygod! I'm talking to the *producer of Almost Making It!*. That's my favorite show on television!"

Everyone stopped and looked up. Paula spied Ralph giving her a really dirty look. It was his "you are hogging the spotlight" look.

She didn't care. She wanted the celebrity now in this unfamiliar group of people. She felt included and relevant. "Yes. This is our vacation. And we chose to spend it this way." Although she smiled, she felt really stupid about her comment about choosing.

"That must be so exciting!"

Paula nodded and waited for the next exclamation, but there was none. Everyone went right back on talking about their gurus. So she studied Antonio and didn't let her disappointment show. He seemed to be an updated version of Ricky Ricardo on *I Love Lucy*, gold chains and all.

"These people are right out of central casting," Paula whispered to Ralph.

"Where does this guy get off bringing *two* women?"

He was thinking about how he could get out of this mess. Even with his cell phone, there was no calling radius. Could he hide out in the room instead of continuing this farce? He *could* get sick. Well, actually, it was too easy to make himself sick. All he had to do was think about the interminable time he was wasting when he could be at work, sorting out office politics and trying to undermine those young Turks on his floor.

He looked into Paula's eyes. She had that feisty, determined look she sometimes got. It was her "Don't-Start-With-Me" stare. Even the beeper on his belt didn't work in this terrain. He was trapped. Could he risk disappointing Paula?

Paula looked back at him and grinned. We are here for the duration, said her smile, and I dare you to leave now.

I have walked into another time warp, she concluded. The group seemed like people who were a little undone by life. On the way out, Ralph grabbed at a flyer that was sitting between two salt shakers on the table. He read aloud from the paper into Paula's ear. "Are you tired of chasing weak orgasms?" He looked at Paula. She was glowering back at him. "Do you feel deeply loved when you have sex?"

The couple who ran the workshop, Sky Spacious and Yogianni Joy, were carefully posed facing toward the camera while they twisted their necks to blissfully look into each other's eyes. The only time Ralph saw people looking like that was when they were political running mates. He read on:

"We will explore these important subjects: Freeing the Female Orgasm, 1001 Methods of Pelvic Movement, The Truth About Amrita (female ejaculation)."

"God, Paula, I am stumped," Ralph whispered into her ear. "In a million years I wouldn't have been able to even formulate the questions to be answered about what was missing in my sex life."

Paula gave him a dirty look.

When Ralph got horny, he gave Paula "The Signal." They had established a code over the years. He would begin caressing her buttocks or just touch her arm unexpectedly. She'd get up and prepare, come back to bed with KY jelly, and they did it. Then they raided the refrigerator. What could be difficult about this? Was this a pass /fail course? Of course, you could make a study of anything, but The Ralph Neuman System had never failed.

Ralph scowled at her. Lately, he felt like a fix-it project instead of a person. At that moment, the look on Ralph's face told Paula that maybe she had gone too far this time. Would he just split?

8

"I'm not going through with this!" Ralph hissed.

He had dragged Paula to the garden just before the beginning of the workshop. His irritation was a contrast to the growth of tender lettuce, basil and shoots of oregano that stood in careful little rows on either side of the stone walk leading to the workshop.

Ralph was no fool. The faces he saw before him at dinner seemed slack with a stress-free life. He was used to eyes full of purpose and intent belonging to people who were seeking destinies of great importance. He had rubbed elbows with captains of industry. However, the visages before him at dinner were flaccid from too much sun, salt and outdoor living. What could they possibly teach him? He had survived in the dog-eat-dog world of corporate life for many years. In that world, a minute was all a man often got to size up another man and his intentions before his head was handed to him and his career ruined. Among his friends and co-workers he saw some creative and gifted men and women, but many of them also were bores and fools, and he had often made the mistake of listening to them open-heartedly, all with equal attention. He ascribed his lack of discrimination to decency and Christian love, but most of the time it had all ended badly. These people at dinner were legends in their own minds due to too much heat, lack of outside stimulation and too much sun. Maybe it was true that sun rots a brain. He had lost his objectivity and compassion somewhere along the way; in his worse moments he thought that maybe he never had any to start with. Maybe he had succumbed to the mediocrity he had fought against all his life. All he knew was that the mosquitoes were biting and he wanted to go home before he came down with something fatal.

If Paula had been observant, she would have noticed Ralph's uncharacteristic cranky look. However, Paula, standing not more than twelve inches away, was running her own movie. It was early evening and she was enjoying the sounds of the birds settling down for the night. It seemed to her that every Bird of Paradise was in bloom on this island, and the lingering light from the day and the viridian ferns enjoined her to gaze at the setting sun. The clouds formed an umbrella of fuchsia and cerulean blue. She could almost walk on the water into the horizon. But in the back of her mind there was a suspicion that some things were imperfectly concealed, and that this was an hour of horror, a naked horror. She knew the shit was going to hit the fan. It did not appear that it was working out with our Ralph. There was nothing to do but pray, and this she did in the most direct fashion: "Oh-shit-God-help; Oh-shit-God-help." This was her mantra.

"Well, you sure did it this time," Ralph snarled. "I'm not feeling so well after that abortion of a supper, and those people are very suspect. I wish you had consulted me before you got us into this thing. I'm not a self-improvement project for you, you know."

He bent down to slap an invisible mosquito that may have landed on his leg. It, if it existed, fled unscathed. Then he slammed the side of his neck and arm, but nothing was there, except a big red welt inflicted by its owner.

"I'm going to get Dengue Fever from these damn mosquitoes, and do you know how far the nearest reliable hospital is around here? No. You don't." He waved his hands in the air and pointed south. "Well, I do. They would have to airlift me from this rain forest to Miami. I could be dead by then. Time enough to make the morning CNN headlines."

"Honey, don't prejudge. This might just be the thing for us," Paula said, thinking of Dr. Jacobs' words. She was in despair. Ralph was so uncompromising sometimes. She vacillated between feeling frightened of abandonment and willfully wanting her own way. She had once told a close girl friend, "If you think marriage is bad, try divorce!" She feared the heavy feelings of estrangement and alienation. Most of all, she was afraid of the shame and failure of her dreams. She knew fifty-year-old divorced women in Marin. They ran from meditation group to support groups to tennis to Hospice to Spanish lessons. They were really spinners. It was not good to be single after fifty, but what fun was it living with someone like Ralph? All the good men had been taken and worked on to a fine finish by their spouses. Only the incorrigible ones were dumped back into the singles heap. Witness the over-fifty singles scene at Strawberry Lagoon Tennis Club on a Friday night. Every George Costanza and Monica Lewinsky were there sucking the energy out of the room. Had she pushed him too far this time? Her willfulness kicked in and she straightened her shoulders. No, she hadn't!

"I have needs, too," she said. "I need this time away. We need quality time together. Only when you suggest something do we do it. It's your couple-friends, your vacation ideas and your parents for Christmas. Well, I want my turn to enjoy something that I've recommended."

"Why do you need a break? I'm the one working eighty hours a week trying to just keep my job from thirty-year-olds trying to steal it out from under me every day. They even wear those disgusting tee shirts to work on Casual Friday that say, 'He who dies with the most toys wins.' Can you imagine?"

"Well, I'm so discouraged with my writing. I just need to get some perspective, and so do you. This will give us something to do while I'm waiting to hear whether my book is going to be sold. I hate this waiting!"

"Sometimes I think you think more about your career than you think of me!"

"Oh, really, then why the hell would I set this up?"

She wondered if he was right. Just what was the normal balance between work and relationships? Because they didn't have kids, she believed that they each threw themselves into work, giving it their fair share of creativity and time that they would have reserved for kids or family sacrifices.

Nonetheless, she was tired of being the person behind the scenes finding those deadbeat celebrities. She felt like the Mother Theresa of has-beens, trying to breathe life back into their already deflated careers and sometimes drug-hazed lives.

She dreamed of becoming famous herself. She knew the publishing market was tight, but she always entertained the possibility that when she walked down the street, people would know her and greet her like some of the icons of Hollywood: Cher, Meryl Streep or Demi Moore. She wouldn't care about paparazzi, "just bring them on." She would know how to handle them. She wanted *her* star on the Hollywood Walk of Fame, and she definitely wanted to be a regular on *Oprah* for her books, her program and her celebrity. She could be the female celebrity of what? Show business? Celebrity sightings? Whatever.

"You'll get on *Oprah*! I know it! Then you'll become famous and leave me behind," Ralph said.

It was just like Ralph to read her mind. She was exasperated by now.

"Oh, stop it."

"You'll get famous, Mrs. Achieve-insky here, and dump me. The man who stood by you all these years." Mrs. Achieve-insky was Ralph's favorite name for Paula when he was angry at her.

"I wasn't exactly a little girl selling pencils at the entrance to Yosemite National Park when you met me, you know. If I get famous, wouldn't you follow me from city to city on my book tours?"

Paula remembered her shock when she went to one of her favorite author's lunchtime readings at a local bookstore. She had found a seat in the back of a crowded room. She thought the audience would be readers and fans. As the question and answer period started, she realized that almost all the hundred women and two men there were wannabe writers. They asked questions not about the content of Amanda Wright's novel, but things like, "Where do you find your plots? How do you develop characters? How do you find time to write? What's your writing schedule?" Questions like these propelled Paula right out the door.

"Sure, I'll even carry your bags," Ralph said sarcastically.

"I'd go on book tours if it was your book."

"No you wouldn't, you'd be flying all over with your work and leave no room for me. Remember the time I was gone to a stupid conference, and I came home and you had flown off in search of Tiny Tim? I was the one who had to let out the dog and feed the cat. They had almost died of starvation, and so did I while you were gone. Our beloved cat Buffy's eyes were rolling in his head with thirst!"

All she really wanted was some recognition of her talents, but it seemed that as she got older she was insatiable for that recognition, or maybe the competition was just greater as younger brilliant women came up the ranks and left her in the dust. They were barking at her heels.

And speaking of recognition, she had even bought a black BMW, top of the line, for just that, come to think of it. Her ego did need feeding at the time. After attending parties, sometimes she would scan the parking lot to see if indeed she still had the most distinctive car there. Often she did, or was a close second.

However, after that book reading, she remembered feeling ordinary and uncreative as she scanned the lot for her black BMW and found it was only one of several dozen. She took out her car keys and pushed the remote button. As her car blinked its headlights in recognition and the door locks popped open, so did several other cars' locking systems that happened to be parked in her vicinity. Even her choice of car, billed as "the ultimate driving machine," was unremarkable.

Snookie told her, "Everyone is an author these days! You can't live in Marin County unless you've written at least one book. You have to have a mailing list, an on-line Zine and a workshop. In fact, at any given moment in Marin, at any location, a writer, psychotherapist or real estate agent is standing only two feet away. It's like that six degrees of separation thing."

Paula had even told Ralph, "I saw this researcher on *Oprah* who was investigating women who live below the poverty line. She spent two years waitressing and living penniless in a trailer park. She also moved around the country working as a cleaning lady and a teacher's aide. At one point she told Oprah that she said in frustration, and at risk of revealing her true identity to her coworkers, 'Unlike you, I can go home and finish my book.' The women looked at her in disbelief and said, 'We're writing books too.'"

Ralph scowled at Paula and she saw how upset he was becoming with her. She wasn't making any headway. When he got like this it was best to exhibit some self-control.

He said, "I feel like you are getting ahead of me. They're all in the pursuit of power, status and money. They've unbridled their greed and ambition. In my work, everyone wants to unseat me. I have to constantly keep my eye on the ball. Fifty-year-old creative directors are an oxymoron! I feel like I'm losing my edge, my ideas are drying up, and every day some other part of my body goes bad."

Paula's spirits sank like a stone. Here they were thousands of miles away from home and he was going at her full blast. She threw caution to the winds. She had to defend herself. She attacked.

"God, you are competitive with me. You are the most difficult man! And if I *did* have a best seller?" You'd probably just go on with your life and wouldn't even come to the readings and tours with me, would you? Does it always have to be the Ralph Neuman Show?"

Sometimes, they had to negotiate before an event who was going to have the top billing, so that Paula, who had a habit of taking over, would exhibit some self-control. Ralph would use his code by saying, "Tonight is the Ralph Neuman show, not the Paula Neuman show."

Paula said, "I never go to dinner parties where your friends ask me what I do for a living? Why, even after women's liberation, it's always the Ralph Neuman show. When is it going to be the Paula Shaw Neuman show? Snookie had to divorce her eighth husband to finally come into her own."

"Oh, so now she is alone, but she has the Snookie McGants show!" Ralph countered vehemently.

"Why is it that women have to support their men? We have to be the wind beneath your wings, but men never think of supporting their women in their creative endeavors unless it is someone like Joan Collins who gets bilked by her latest boy husband or Liz Taylor and her latest alimony-rich blue-collar husband. You know what I mean."

"How can you say that? I have logged in hundreds of man-hours attending networking parties for your business. Do you think it is any fun when people come up to me knowing I am your husband and call me Ralph Shaw?"

"Oh, right. You come in and greet everyone and then take your cell phone or go into the host's library or kitchen and make phone calls to your clients and we never see you again until it is time to leave. A *real* partner would stand by my side and smile so I could introduce you. No one even knows who you are because of your antics. You don't have a clue as to what wind beneath my wings really means, much less feels like!" She stomped her foot.

It had grown dark. They could only see each other's outlines from the lights in the seminar room.

"Well, I may need to leave and have my own vacation."

"Is that a threat?"

Ralph had never behaved this way before and it frightened Paula. Usually they came to some compromise in the end. All the other times one or the other had given in, and they had softened and embraced, declared their undying love and caring. But this was not happening tonight.

"No, it's not a threat unless *you* see it as one, but I want you to know I don't like this and unless I change my mind, I will find other ways to occupy my time. Remember when I am dying in an airlift out of here with Dengue Fever, you were the one who arranged the whole thing. Why didn't you just leave out a plate of arsenic?"

"You'd think you could be happy that I signed us up for this, thinking of our marriage, but no, you only think of yourself. You think you could feel happy for me if I get to be the on the best seller list instead of complaining?"

"I'd be happy for you if I didn't think I was going to lose you to stardom and The Oprah Circuit. Well, I hope you get your fifteen minutes of fame."

"Very funny. Well, write your own novel then. Stop complaining." Paula stomped off.

"You'll see," yelled Ralph. "You're going to get a run for your money! I'll show you!"

The sun had set and the path was pitch black. Paula wished that she had tempered her remarks because she was frightened about what Ralph would do next. She often regretted that she couldn't keep her own promises to herself about just keeping her mouth shut and not escalating things.

9

Miracle prepared the machine to do the colonic. It had to be clean and sterile. On this balmy day in Paradise, she thought about her move from Palm Beach, Florida, where she first learned this skill. With each new move — a critical care center in Arizona, a nursing home in California, and finally, six months ago, a flight to Tortola, British Virgin Islands, she dreamed of meeting a rich man who would take care of her.

She rented this office from Dr. Moskowitz, the chiropractor next door. They shared a common waiting room. This afternoon she thought about her cloying mother and single younger sister, Sheba. Miracle left them in Florida on her thirty-second birthday. Her life was going nowhere. It was sun bathing by the condo pool, bridge games, rictus smiles of old men and their open-necked shirts to exhibit their gold chains, and rooming with her cynical, overweight older sister.

Delila, the only friend she had on the island, told her that this was where wealthy men spent their time. Delila had met one of them already.

"The place is filthy with them," Delila told her, "on the beach, in hotels and, an extra bonus, the beaches are all public!"

Hoping for the best, she had adopted Delila's vacation lifestyle.

"How is it in Paradise?" her sister asked snidely when she called on Sunday night. "Have you found a husband yet? Have you bought a bikini? How much weight have you lost?"

Miracle felt defeated. In her studio condo on she sweltered at night. She drowned her sadness in boxes of Snackwell shortbreads and Vandange Chardonnay that she bought at the ABC store a block away.

The only exercise she got was walking there after work to pick up her evening's worth of food and drink. It was also her only form of entertainment. She called it "face entertainment." She gave all her Florida bathing suits to the Sunburst Consignment Store in hopes of getting a new start on life. The suits looked old and stretched-out compared to the landscape of smooth skin stretched over taut bodies that was displayed on the beach here in Paradise.

She was forty pounds overweight and gaining rapidly. There was nothing else to do after the sun went down in this island town but watch television and snack, unless you had a husband and a family.

As she changed the sheets on her therapy table and waited for the next client, a streak of resentment ran through her. She had mixed feelings about her sister and her mother. On the one hand, she felt sad being so far from home, yet she resented them for their obvious opinions about her life.

She answered a knock on the door that signaled her fifth and final client today. The referrals from the hotel were usually peri-menopausal women who were constipated or old codgers with their caretakers. They discussed their condition before they got on the table as "blockages," and their bodily functions as "evacuation" or "pressing problems."

Her mentor, Dr. Solsky, stressed to her that elimination was the road to illumination. She had this inscribed on a framed plaque in her closet that Dr. Solsky gave all his students after their certification program.

Because she transposed numbers and letters frequently, she was forced to drop out of college after one semester. This was the only profession she could get into without taking a test.

The man who walked through her door was not her usual type of client. He was about ten years older than Miracle and wore cowboy boots and an expensive wide-brim hat on his six-foot- five sturdy frame. She had written Reefdancer Schwartz in her appointment book.

When she was nervous, her coin-colored eyes got wide and frozen in her head and her voice got sugary like butter-brickle candy. She was nervous now.

"Before we begin, I'd like to take a brief history, if you don't mind?" She shuffled her papers on her clipboard and found an empty form. This was how she learned to do it in the Colonic Hygiene School of Medicine in Palm Beach.

The breeze from the ocean floated through her open windows and she smelled the salt air that signaled the tide was going out. A slightly fishy smell tingled in her nostrils. She thought absentmindedly about what she would buy for supper as soon as this session was over.

"Asking these questions helps settle the client and build rapport and trust in a vulnerable situation," Dr. Solsky had said. He wasn't a real medical doctor, he was a chiropractor, but he had been the only mentor she ever had. Her dad had abandoned the family when she was six. Her mom supported them by working as a cleaning lady in motels along the beach towns that dotted the East coast from New Jersey to Miami, where they finally ended up and made a home.

"Have you had a colonic before?" Miracle looked into this man's open and indisputably handsome face. She smelled the pleasant scent of his after-shave lotion.

It was disgusting when some patients came unwashed straight from the beach with their saltwater sticky skin and slathers of sun block still sticking to their midriffs. But she had come to expect that from any beach town.

"Yes," he said. "When I lived in Palm Beach."

Miracle stopped and put the pen down. She looked into his face. My God, she thought. This man was different. He smelled good and he looked wonderful. She woke up from her indifferent stupor, straightened her shoulders and put a scintillating smile on her face for the first time that day.

"That's where I came from," she squealed, and grinned.

She could feel herself being inextricably drawn to this man she knew nothing about and wishing that he would find her attractive too. How could he? Was that even possible? The box of chocolate crème Snackwell's cookies lay heavy in her stomach from the night before. She felt bloated and filled with self-loathing from her noonday meal. She just knew he wouldn't find her attractive. Determined to act professionally, she composed herself again.

"Well, since you've done this before, you know then that it won't hurt," she reassured him. "Just undress and climb on the table. Please drape yourself. When you are done, ring this little bell and I'll return to flush you out."

She handed him a clean white sheet and left the room. She stood outside in the waiting room, nervous and feeling silly about this attraction.

Shortly, Miracle heard the bell and slipped back into the quiet room.

Now a slight wind came up, as it often did in the afternoons. She walked to the window and closed it slightly. "It may be too cool on you, as we begin to work," she said.

He turned and noticed her round hips and buttocks. He knew that it wouldn't be hard to seduce this woman. He had done it many times before, with his sad stories.

She noticed him noticing, and smiled.

"Now if you would turn to the left side." She assisted him making sure the drape was discreetly over all the important parts of his body. But she couldn't help noticing his tanned skin and his washboard stomach. It was the body of a man who did a lot of physical labor.

Once the sheet was over his torso, she couldn't help but take a moment to admire his muscular buns. An unanticipated wave of sexual longing flushed through her.

Carefully, she took out several other clean white sheets and draped him so just the area where she could work was exposed.

"You'll feel a slight pinching," she said as she inserted the rubber end of a long tube. The rest of the tubing opened into a clear glass pipe no wider than three inches that ran from his body into the drain in the sink.

She turned on the machine and the room was filled with a slight whirling noise. She reached over to hold his hand, a typical procedure for a new client.

"Now relax your bowel, as if you are evacuating, and the machine will do the rest."

Reefdancer smiled up at her, comforted by her presence. He smelled the incense that cleansed the room, and the air from the beach that was so familiar on this part of the island, and it soothed him. That afternoon, in the coolness of her office, Miracle sat quietly beside her client. As the detritus of the colon and lower intestines flushed and floated past them both through the glass tube, they watched with mild interest. For a few moments they were silent, the way people are when they meditate or are comforted by the presence of the other. Finally Miracle spoke.

"Where in Florida do you come from?"

"Palm Beach. My family came from Miami. That's where I was born, but I grew up in Palm Beach." Lying on the Egyptian cotton sheets, with nothing to do but gaze at the flow of bodily fluids, he turned his attention to her and began to share.

"My dad was a mortgage broker, but he was very religious."

"You mean mortgage brokers aren't religious?"

He picked up his head to get a better look at her. He noticed her quick smile and the laugh lines around her mouth. And then he laughed.

"No, no, that's not what I meant!"

She laughed too, and continued, "Jewish?"

"Yeah, I'm Jewish, how did you know?"

"Well, Schwartz is a Jewish name. When you called to make the appointment."

She bent her head down closer to him, as if to confide something.

"I am, too."

"Oh, of course." He laughed and looked up into her eyes. He always filled out applications as "Reefdancer" Morris Schwartz. His real name felt like a relic of the past.

"I use Reefdancer now. I guess when I'm in the doctor's office I'm still in the habit of writing down the name on my birth certificate, you know." He shrugged his shoulders and lay his head down again on the table.

She liked the way he laughed. It was deep and throaty, as if he enjoyed himself. Then he raised himself on his elbows and continued.

"We were pretty well off. I was the only son and my dad's favorite. Actually, we lived really way over our means and had servants."

"Servants?" Miracle echoed him, and then she felt stupid. She scolded herself to keep her mouth shut and just listen.

"By the age of ten, I'd gone to Cuba and Europe. So I knew that I was better off than most kids."

She found him very talkative, unlike most of her other patients, but she didn't want him to stop. Usually, she would say, "It's time to just lie still and enjoy this, Mr. or Mrs. So-and-So." But she didn't want him to ever stop. He had whetted her curiosity, so she asked him the kinds of questions that Delila had told her gave you a lot of information about who people are.

She leaned over and asked in a nonchalant way, "What do you do here on the island?"

"I own a horse ranch and farm. "

"Wow!" was all she could say. Then she caught her breath. It just didn't compute that Jews rode horses. This was not part of *her* life experience growing up in the same exact place in Florida. She only knew Jews read books or wrote books, invented things or played the violin. Her family was an exception, of course, because they were very poor. A Jewish cowboy? She wanted to learn more.

"How in the world did you learn about horses?"

"My dad taught me polo at the country club we belonged to. Well, there were clubs that Jews couldn't belong to, so he started one just for Jews. Did you know the Palm Beach Tennis and Racquet Club?"

"Oh, I heard of it," she said. Well, she had never heard of it, but she supposed that was the thing to say to keep the conversation going. That's what Delila would have done.

"I went on polo tournaments. That was before Dad got into the habit of gambling."

Miracle had never been around gamblers before. It seemed so exciting that his dad was a gambler. She didn't even *know* her dad.

"A gambler?"

"Yeah, he loved everything about horses, especially racing. Eventually he got arrested embezzling some money from his associates in the business community so he could use it to pay his gambling debts. The cops actually came to our estate and handcuffed him and arrested him."

Miracle's stomach flip-flopped. She didn't know what was worse, a dad who abandoned his child, or a dad who was arrested. Well, maybe it was just about the same thing. Both involved the disappointment in another human being who was supposed to take care of you.

"How old were you?" She reached out and touched his arm. She was wondering if he had been very young and vulnerable like she had been when her dad left.

"Oh about thirteen, at the time."

"What happened to you and your family? I mean how did they live?" she asked. She was thinking that they went into a downward spiral like her mom and sister.

"Well, then they had this big sensational trial, the family name was plastered all over the Palm Beach *Herald*. No one would talk to me at school. Our family became pariahs in the town. You probably were too young to read about it," he said, referring to their obvious age difference.

"What a horrible thing to have happen in your life," Miracle sighed, and continued to watch absent-mindedly as the tube carried deposits into the sink and plumbing beyond.

Reefdancer sighed too and put his head back down on the table. He moved the pillow closer to prop himself up in a more comfortable position. "Dad was sent to a maximum-security prison in Arkansas, and Mom and I had to take a train and three buses to visit him every two weeks for the next ten years. He really put the family through hell, and I grew to hate him."

Reefdancer seemed so small and vulnerable to her. So much had happened in the short time he had been in the office.

"How awful," she crooned. She wanted to show concern for his difficult life and let him know that she was an emotionally giving person.

"My high school life was ruined because of it, and I vowed never to do any mean-spirited thing to destroy others or to get even."

She loved hearing him talk about his inner life. She felt so close to him.

She straightened the sheet near his head and said, "Did you ever make up with your dad?"

"Not really, because the final straw was that when I was sixteen, I found out that I had a half brother from another marriage. Can you believe that he had lied to my mother and me for years? He was supporting another family that we didn't know about until much later!"

Reefdancer's voice grew louder. Miracle could tell that he still had a charge on this part of his story. She wondered what it would be like to be a real therapist and get people to talk about their lives like Reefdancer was doing now. She knew that she would be good at it.

"Oh my God, how did you ever find that out?"

"This fat kid, about eight years older than I, showed up at the prison one day with the same last name. I was so angry. The first chance I got, after I got my driver's license, I drove out to California."

"Where?"

"Oh, Marin County."

"Me, too, I lived in Marin," she squealed. It seemed miraculous that someone else lived in Marin at one time besides Miracle, the way it does when you are so far away from home and someone knows the same person you do. I mean, what are the odds?

"Yeah? But I couldn't find any work. I really didn't know how to do anything except live off the money I had saved. So finally, I flew to Tortola. I was so depressed after six months that one afternoon I just walked into the ocean."

"Oh my God, you poor man," said Miracle. "Don't ever even think of that. Things can get pretty bad in life, but never do that."

He smiled at her. Maybe it was her innocence or her naïveté that caught him. He thought her comment was cute and so unpretentious.

"I know, I know." He reached for her hand to reassure her. "I was determined to drown myself. I got out pretty far, and the waves were really rolling that day, and I knew that I could never swim back. I was a goner and I was so frightened."

Miracle listened intently. Caught up in the drama of the story, she forgot to lessen the pressure of the valve.

"Suddenly, I saw a woman swimming towards me. I mean she was a *good* swimmer and she dragged me to shore. It must have been over two miles out, but she did it. And that was Yogianni."

"Yogianni?"

Miracle suddenly remembered and reached over to slow down the flow, but she sensed some disappointment brewing right around the corner of her mind. Did he have a girlfriend? Was he married? Was all this too good to be true? Will I ever see him again?

"She and Sky are my family."

"Your family? I thought your family was back on the East Coast?"

"No, you know, my extended family. Yogianni and Sky, they are together."

He lifted his index and middle finger and put them together to demonstrate a couple.

Silently, Miracle breathed a sigh of relief.

Maybe it was the intimacy of the colonic itself that led to revealing secrets, maybe it was the relief and warm sensation of water clearing an impacted area, maybe it was because they both were astrological water signs, but as his bowels were releasing and clearing, he was also expunging his past, and with it his hopes, dreams and desires, to this sweet, ample-breasted, dark-haired beauty.

Reefdancer told Miracle everything. She took his hands and looked into his hazel eyes. At that moment, she wanted to heal not only his bowels, but also all his wounds.

She climbed onto the table beside him after his session was over and they quietly made love, especially slowly, so her chiropractor landlord wouldn't hear them. Years later she would realize that this act gave new meaning to Dr. Solsky's prophetic words which reverberated in her head that day: Illumination through elimination.

Miracle had never done anything like this before with a client. She had standards, but she knew in her heart that this man was someone set apart. He was different.

He was wise and sophisticated and instinctively, she knew that he would lead her to her dreams of a vacation life style and a wedding that would be the envy of her sister. He loved her slowly and well, unlike her first husband, the plumber, who was rough and fast, with dirty nails and fingers like sides of beef.

He loved her zaftig body under his hands. He kneaded her thighs and buttocks. He believed that he had never felt anyone or anything with such soft, yielding skin. Not even his young mares felt so good.

The next day he introduced her to his support group, and to Sky and Yogianni. Immediately, she became part of his ready-made family and thus began her life in Paradise.

"They will teach you to become a Tantriki Goddess," Reefdancer said. Sky and Yogianni have been living together, and once a week Sky declares a day of Autonomy, where he goes with three of his tantrikis and they do G spot work all day."

"How does Yogianni feel about this?" asked Miracle with amazement.

"She gets to interview each of them to be sure they pay perfect homage to her," Reefdancer said. Shortly after, he enrolled Miracle and himself in her first weekend, where Paula and Ralph sat across from them.

When Reefdancer, a.k.a. Morris Schwartz, walked out of Miracle's office after that session and looked out to the western sky, he had never seen the sun setting more brilliantly, and he knew he had gotten more than a colonic from this Tortola Goddess.

10

We all know people like Annabelle Anne Smith from Wichita, Kansas. They are the meat and potatoes personalities of the world and they come from the Midwestern meat, fats and carbohydrate diets of parents and grandparents who drove across the country in covered wagons. You can still see the rutted remnants of wagon wheel tracks in the rocks if you stop in Laramie or Jackson Hole. The pioneers are the sisters and cousins of faceless relations we all know, but who have moved away. We hear about them from our relatives at holidays and family gatherings after the food and drink have taken effect. Our bellies are full and all the local gossip is wrung dry.

"Oh, and Annabelle," cousin Ruth might say. "Well, would you believe it? She's moved to the British Virgin Islands after a stop in California, and she's even taken a new name. She never writes or calls. She's taken up with a sort of cult from what cousin Dwayne has told me. I never thought that girl would get her life back together after her husband ran off with her older sister."

Ears perk up and heads lean forward at the holiday table. A tidbit of gossip to chew on; in our hearts, someone we don't wish well, one of the clan who escaped the herd mentality. They got away, and secretly we know that doesn't bode well for us.

"I've never seen anything like that around these parts before. She hardly had any talents for the sewing or planting, the way her two other sisters did. What *could* she have done to have her husband run off like that?"

"Her father sure ruled that family with an iron hand. Maybe if he had let those girls go to college, things might have turned out differently."

And so the conversation goes. If her relatives were flies on the wall, wouldn't they be surprised to discover that her only gift, her sexuality, served her well and has taken her farther than even she dreamed?

Would they be surprised that she was the co-author of a book on Tantric sex? Would they have read the book she wrote with Sky Spacious if they had found it on a shelf in the library? Or would they categorize it with pornography and smut?

Would they be astonished to find out that Annabelle Anne Smith a.k.a. Yogianni was a very big fish in another small pond called Tortola? She is the star and centerpiece of her own colorful world. But this wasn't a postcard she could write home about, since she hadn't spoken to her family in five long years. Not since she was humiliated by the events that gave her notoriety in Wichita. Nor has she spoken to her sisters or father.

Is it by destiny or conscious choice that we find our next partner in this fast-paced world? And are they repeats from the past? Can one ever get past feeling like one is living with parts of one's father or mother's emotional landscape? Yogianni wondered about that on this particular day. If she had been born just a hundred years before, in her little town, there would be only a few available men to choose from. Lucky for her, she thought, as she put their workshop materials together and waited for Sky, her partner, that she had more range of choice in this lifetime. What luck she had found Sky. Actually, Sky had chosen her.

Her musings were becoming unpleasant, because Sky was three hours late, and she was growing angrier by the minute.

By noon her anger had turned to despair. Humidity and the becalmed ocean set her on edge. The grayish pink smog coming from the sugar mill hung like a ribbon cloud over the Sage Mountains.

From her vantage point high above the surf and the bay, she could smell the ocean as the tide went out. She was developing yet another migraine headache from the intense late afternoon heat.

Yesterday was Sky's Autonomy Day. That was the day he chose to sleep with one of his other women under the watchful eye of Yogianni. But he hadn't come home last night. That wasn't part of the deal they had struck after much vexation and tension that kept surfacing in their rocky relationship.

From the time she was a young girl, she had been told by her two sisters that she was not very attractive, an unremarkable person in every way. The older sister could sing and dance, and the younger one could write and act, but by the age of eleven, the whole family agreed that Annabelle Anne Smith was indeed ordinary as a cow, far as anyone could tell.

That was the only thing the whole volatile family agreed upon. Most of the time she got no feedback. Her irascible alcoholic father ruled the house with an iron hand. He was the king in his castle of courtesans. Why send her to college when she was only going to get married and have kids?

By the time we meet her, Annabelle had grown tallish in her appearance, and had an interesting, chiseled face with big blue eyes. Thinly disguised behind her scintillating and feminine presence was a manipulative, approval-seeking woman.

Her "college education" was *Cosmopolitan* magazine. She read it from cover to cover from the time she discovered that the buds on her chest were the early growth of some small, unremarkable looking nipples and breasts.

Cosmopolitan came in the mailbox and was grabbed first by her mother and handed down from mother to sister to sister to her. It was dog-eared by the time she learned the latest techniques of blending eye shadow or the "snap-and-spring" method to get a man's attention. She learned to intentionally drop something on the floor, bend over letting her breasts separate, and then spring up while running her hands along her sides, using them as pointers or guides for the man's eyes to follow. She and her sisters practiced this for weeks until they got it exactly right. She also learned how to walk and stand the European woman's way, with one leg in front of the other and her toe pointed and slightly extended.

The behavior of her husband and sister had made her wary of other women. After she found him in bed with her sister, she couldn't trust any woman not to steal any man she might love. To save face in the family and community, she first ran off to California and then to Tortola.

She longed for a man to find something in her and draw it out, since she was convinced of her lack of worth. That was until Sky found her eating tofu at the food bar in Rainbow Foods. Their meeting was by chance and he found her unremarkable in every way. He only remembered her later because she spilled a jug of soymilk all over him at the checkout stand.

Then suddenly, his latest tantriki had flown the coop back to the mainland. It occurred to him that she might even have crossed paths with Annabelle Anne Smith, but that was before he renamed her and made her over into Yogianni, his beloved new assistant. She developed a manner of being docile, accommodating and very suggestible. Hidden from view, she nursed her many longings and practiced her quiet manipulations.

She was just the right person for him. He found her insecure about her own worth and still trying to figure out what she wanted to be as an adult. With his coaching, she became the star of his Tantric seminars. In return for being his protégée, she had to allow him his freedom, "To practice what I preach," he had said.

"Why won't you marry me?" she accused him after living and working hard for him for several months. She dreamed of going to nursing school, of being a housewife, of ironing hankies and waxing floors. She was fascinated by how straight people lived. She longed to decorate her own house and have children.

"I'm not ready yet," he said. He knew that he would probably never be ready, and he had bluffed and stalled for years with women just like her. "Why buy the cow when you can get the milk for free?" her mother would have said to her if she had known about the current situation.

Sky was a strange-looking man with a big round face and a short and dense body. From some angles and lighting, he had eyes like a goat: his pupils appeared like sideway slits, amber-colored and gray.

Sky didn't seem to mind Yogianni's activities with other couples, it just added extra income for them. As long as he wasn't married to her, he didn't care who she slept with. His commitment was for his work life only. She was like his trained trick puppy. Of course, he knew it wouldn't be forever.

Women were wild about him. They surrounded him like women surround a rock star. He exuded pheromones, an invisible sexual substance that targeted all women with vaginal longing that could only be satisfied by touch, but his biggest secret was that he was more interested in satisfying the woman than in satisfying himself. In fact, he got great pleasure out of it, the way a maestro controls his orchestra. Therefore, his reputation preceded him, and women lined up at his front door to have a try, orgasmic and non-orgasmic women alike.

When Sky first came to the island he joined the Urobionimist clan, hoping that since this was an island and water was a limited resource, he could eventually take over leadership of the practice of drinking and washing in one's own urine. The philosophy interested him as well. Their members believed that urine, high in nutrients, was naturally nutritious. But the craze never caught on, and the interest in the clan died out. It may have been the fragrance emitted when mixed with bodily heat. It was so malodorous, women's interest dropped off. He abandoned the idea completely. But he was a good son, and he discreetly sent his mother several thousand dollars each month, revenues from his Tantric Sex Workshops, so she could live in style in Miami.

As with all workshop leaders and their partners, they had to have a loving public image if they were to earn a living and live in the manner to which they wanted to be accustomed but had never really experienced. So Sky and Yogianni had developed a tacit agreement that they both had no past except with each other, that there was no danger in their paradise that a little sexual debriefing couldn't cure, and that their island and their work protected them from all the fear and trouble in the world. They lived in a cocoon of love and enlightenment.

Privately, though, Yogianni was becoming tired of his behavior. An impression was taking shape in her mind. Lately, it seemed to her that anyone on Tortola who was into enlightenment thought Sky was the Alpha Dog of sex. This made her feel insecure. In fact, their circle tried to outdo each other as to who was more enlightened and spiritual.

It was late that evening and dark when Yogianni picked up the phone. Sky still hadn't returned. But she wasn't calling one of her girlfriends. She couldn't reveal her pain; she had a reputation to keep. Then she put the receiver down again. It was unusual even for Sky to return so late on his Autonomy Day. Could he have really connected with someone this time in a way that had never happened before? Could she continue to go through this abandoned feeling year after year?

It was painful seeing couples who seemed more solid than Sky and herself. Paula and Ralph, whom she'd met the night before at the orientation, really seemed to have it together the way most couples on the island didn't. Could it be, too, that Miracle and Reefdancer were posing a new threat, in that they were getting married, and she still wasn't, after all she had given up and given out?

Luck would have it that Dr. Jacobs was home that night in his condo with a view of San Francisco when Yogianni finally got up her courage to make the call. He answered on the second ring.

"I am delighted to hear from you, my dear! It's been too long," he said. "I really miss you folks. How is the Tantric sex going?"

Yogianni breathed a sigh of relief. She had always put Dr. Jacobs on a pedestal, and she was afraid that he had never really noticed her.

"Well, the island isn't the same without you." She spoke softly and seductively. "I wonder if you could do me a small favor?"

"Sure, anything, my love. You know I always thought you were doing a great service to mankind, or should I say womankind." He laughed heartily.

"I am having some difficulty with Sky right now." She stopped and took a deep breath. "Maybe it is me that I'm having difficulty with. "

It seemed like several years of tears welled up and flooded her eyes. Dr. Jacobs waited for her crying to subside and then she told him everything. She hadn't intended to. Perhaps it was his tender manner, but Dr. Jacobs met her pain with sympathy, empathy and interest.

"I wonder if I could make myself feel more desirable to him. I heard of some kind of estrogen that would cause me to be more, shall I say, interested?"

"Oh, sure Yogianni, I know about that. It's a cream of a certain percent titration that you apply to your vaginal area. It helps keep that area youthful and may raise your libido. Is that what you mean?"

"Exactly."

Dr. Jacobs promised to promptly call in the prescription to Yogianni's local pharmacy. But there was more to the conversation. "You know, if Sky is treating you poorly, you can always come and stay with me."

Yogianni was surprised. "I thought you forgot about me."

Dr. Jacobs paused. He felt a strong attraction to her that had always gone unexpressed.

"My dear, I've always wondered why we weren't closer."

There was silence on the other end of the receiver.

"In fact, if you want to take a, let's say 'moratorium' on your relationship, give me a call. You can stay with me and have some rest and relaxation. We can see how it goes."

Yogianni pictured the life of leisure in his condo in Marin, living with a real doctor. Wouldn't her family back home be taken aback!

"You really mean that?"

"Of course, my dear," Dr. Jacobs said lovingly.

"I really appreciate the offer, but let me sleep on it awhile," said Yogianni. "You are so sweet to want to help me."

"That's what I'm here for, my dear. Call me in the next week or two and let me know how you feel. No pressure." Dr. Jacobs knew that Yogianni was a real stunt pilot in bed, and she would probably not ask much of him otherwise. She seemed desperate and grateful for any acts of kindness. This was his kind of gal.

By late the next morning, Yogianni had been to the pharmacy, slathered herself up with newly purchased estrogen cream, and was waiting for subtle changes to happen. She called Miracle to tell her about her latest discovery. "This stuff would be great for your wedding night."

"No, I can't wait. I may want to test it out first," Miracle said.

Yogianni told herself that she would get better than all these other women Sky was with. She would be his irresistible sex goddess when he arrived. He'd want no other.

As Sky was driving home from his latest sexual encounter with an Asian woman, he was thinking how funny it was, the way couples find each other. Yogianni and he were like bookends. Their backgrounds really mirrored one another in a way. He came from a broken family from the Bronx and had driven a taxi in New York. He studied the high-flying men he picked up at the airport and formed his image around their style and way with women. That was his on-the-job training. When he actually met Yogianni, he knew she was just right for his work. Long ago, he discovered that he could hide his inadequacies by going on the offensive with women and devising an interviewing style. That way he could better control the situation. He was considered the most desirable man in some circles because of his dexterity with his fingers.

He had certainly found his niche in life, which was more than most men could say. He had a real job doing what he loved. Men envied him. He actually could make a living and never leave the comfort of his bed, so to speak.

Just when Yogianni was about to collapse from heat, anxiety and exhaustion, she heard Sky's car come up the gravel driveway.

"Hi, honey. How was your day?" He dropped his beach bag by the door and pecked her on the cheek just like an executive coming home on the commuter train.

She met him with a sweet smile and silence. She knew not to jump him when he first arrived. She'd have more leverage if she waited for the right time. How did other women endure this type of betrayal, she wondered? What was the price she was paying? Jackie Onassis lived with it for a time, and she was *famous*. Then why couldn't she, Yogianni, live with it?

She waited until bedtime, but he didn't come in. Now he was writing something on his computer. When she heard him finish and walk into the other room, she waited several minutes, and then she could wait no longer.

She sidled up to him as he lounged on the sofa watching David Letterman and drinking some chardonnay. She undid his pants. He clicked off the television with the remote and he drew her to him. But after he entered her and the friction started, he came to a screeching halt. Up he jumped off the sofa and screamed, "What did you do, put cayenne pepper on your yoni?"

Yogianni looked up in confusion. Sky's face was filled with outrage.

"All I did was put some estrogen cream on so that I might feel more desirable." She began to sob for the second time that evening because all her good intentions to further his interest were dashed. She collapsed inside.

A firestorm of resentments followed.

"I can't go on like this, you disappear for days and I'm supposed to be okay with it." She whined and raged.

"You don't understand, honey, if I'm to do my work, I need time, like a musician, to perfect my craft." He was feeling constrained, but he knew they had to be in good form for the workshop the next day. He didn't want to get into a hassle before bed.

"It's only you that I love. Think of those other women as just tuning my instrument."

He put his arms around her soothingly. She melted under his touch once more and vowed to live with his indiscretions because he was such an artist. And like most women who are ensconced in an illusion of security, she wondered if there was still time to change him. It was later that she learned from Dr. Jacobs that this type of estrogen should not be used if you plan to have intercourse immediately. Intercourse is unadvisable for twelve hours, or damage can be done.

11

On the first evening of the workshop, Yogianni in the catalogue, a.k.a. Annabelle Anne Smith, and her partner, a former Manhattan taxi cab driver, Sky Spacious, sat cross-legged in the middle of a dimly lit room.

"Tantric sex is the process of transforming the kundalini at the base of the spine into sexual energy throughout the body. In this workshop I promise you spiritual enlightenment through sexual transformation."

They smiled at each other and made eye contact, the way Sam Donaldson did with Diane Sawyer before they closed their show.

Ralph whispered to Paula, "Just how much did you pay for this?"

She ignored his question, but whispered back, "The workshop is open to couples only." She gave him an exaggerated you-know-what-I-mean look.

He smacked the side of his head dramatically and rolled his eyes so that only she could see. It was too late to make a big scene in the midst of all these people. "I can't believe you paid for something like this! At least there won't be any guys pawing each other here." Paula guessed he meant gay men, but when she had signed up that hadn't even crossed her mind. "How much would you think something like this *would* cost, Big Guy?" she hissed.

The catalogue description had caught her eye:

"This workshop offers participants ways to increase intimacy and passion in their relationship not learned in unhealthy childhood experiences. We will free up female sexual hang-ups, and learn about orgasm and methods to increase pleasure for both partners, along with hands-on sexual healing and awakening skills. Esoteric practices of kiss, movement and touch, along with many other exotic lovemaking skills, will be introduced in class, and then practiced in the privacy of your own room. This seminar presents Tantric wisdom with compassion and gentleness."

Yogianni stood up for the first time. Paula gasped at what she was wearing, or not wearing. Yogianni had on a gauzy see-through blouse and floral skirt. Paula thought she could see her thong underpants. Virtual clothes. God, she hoped Ralph wasn't getting turned on to her. It was so blatant.

Her hair was arranged in one of those artfully disheveled up-dos: a lot of stray tendrils framing the jaw, and something like a chopstick piercing a rough bun at the back. It was the sort of hairstyle that film actresses wear when they're playing sexy lady doctors.

Yogianni said, in a sweet, mellifluous tone, "Tantric sex shows us the mysteries of sexual love and energy." She smiled broadly and eyed each face to create the illusion of intimacy. "It is an ancient, esoteric art form. Sexual energy is a vital sacrament that, rightly used, brings great harmony and joy into one's relationship so that love continues to grow over the course of a lifetime, deeply bonding the partners in joyous spiritual union."

She looked around the room. Her eyes landed self-consciously on each person. She made sure she made eye contact with each person and smiled again.

"I want everyone to stand." Yogianni tiptoed over to the wall and slowly turned down the dimmer lights.

The room was filled with the shuffling of nine couples of various dimensions and girths. They moved their knapsacks, purses and water bottles to the side of the room and unfolded their torsos upward to stand. Paula could tell by the tanned skin of the women near her that they seemed younger, or more well preserved than she. They must have spent a lot of time out of doors, not like her, in a windowless office, hustling for the next piece of business. She hoped that once the word got around about what she did, they wouldn't find reasons for a private consultation, take out their resumes and haunt her, as often happened with has-beens.

The men came in all sizes and shapes and were not exactly the business types she and Ralph were so used to.

Paula was making a mental note to call the local tanning salon upon return, when she heard Yogianni clear her throat as a signal that she was about to begin again. Like the obedient student she was, she looked to the front of the room where Yogianni stood.

Yogianni paused respectfully, waiting for the group's attention with a wide, practiced smile pasted on her face. Then she said, "I want the women to find a partner of the opposite sex, not the person you came with, and stand in front of him."

There was a flurry of whispering in the room. Paula looked at Ralph. She wasn't ready to give him up just yet, but before she could decide what to do, a short voluptuous blonde had pushed her out of her place and was standing directly in front of Ralph, smiling at him and introducing herself, ready to go.

Paula felt a sharp pain of jealousy. Everyone had instantly paired up. Where had Paula been?

The only person left was a tall, broad shouldered, blonde-haired man that she thought might be in his late forties. She could tell by his enlarged pupils that fear was raging in his eyes. He kept glancing over at his partner, now fully engaged with Ralph, and not looking into Paula's eyes as he was supposed to do. Paula immediately understood. He was staring at his partner now staring into Ralph's eyes.

Paula felt like she was back in fourth grade and playing musical chairs. Maybe she had been all wrong and too hasty about coming here. Of all the men in the group, Ralph, her very own personal husband, was chosen first. She hadn't realized how marketable he was.

Sky Spacious was speaking from the back of the room. He was wearing a dashiki. Paula flashed on all of Ralph's dashikis she had given to Goodwill on the spur of the moment, in a fit of spring-cleaning. She had really wanted to clean Ralph out of the house that day.

No one ever talks about male menopause, Paula pondered. They stockpile Viagra in secret little out-of-the-way places in the bathroom; they stand in front of the mirror for hours assessing the square footage and rate of thinning hair, or how the accomplishments of other men their age drive them wild with envy.

On the other hand, Sky Spacious did look delicious in his dashiki, despite his thinning hair and pasty skin. He was oozing pheromones. Her manicurist had told her about those little invisible chemicals that men put out in the ozone to attract women. Even men in their sixties have them, she had told her. Paula's lips turned upward in a secret smile. Her manicurist had been looking for an eligible doctor to marry for years. She finally came in under the wire, marrying a Ph.D. Paula wondered if a Ph.D. qualified. Since the marriage, her manicurist had become unbearably psychological. She acted like she had gotten the Ph.D. herself by giving her unsolicited advice during pedicures.

"I want to welcome all the Brotherhood of Gods and the Sisterhood of Goddesses of the Islands," Yogianni said. "You are here because you consciously transcended your programming and want to learn more about how to sexually heal your union with your beloved. Sky Spacious and I met under a destiny star, and were guided to teach what we have explored with each other."

Sky took over. "This weekend you will have an opportunity to practice with each other and have coaching from my Tantriki partner, Yogianni."

Sky Spacious put his arm around his partner, who was swathed in chiffon scarves and barefooted. She tilted slightly towards him on her toes, pushing upward into his face. She seemed like she was about to dance as she smiled into his eyes.

"You may sign up with her throughout the weekend and she will come to your room and give you hands-on pointers as you pleasure your partner. You are in for a treat. One of our couples is blessing us with their wedding vows during this workshop. And this is a first. It is Reefdancer and Miracle, his beloved. He has generously invited you all to their wedding."

Reefdancer stood up and took a fake swashbuckling bow. Paula noted how very attractive he was.

"Miracle will be here later," he announced. "She is healing a client at the hotel."

How provocative, Paula thought. A thrill ran through her, to think they might go to a wedding. What woman didn't love weddings? And then she remembered Ralph. She looked around, but she couldn't see him in the dim light of the room.

Sky dropped his arm from Yogianni's shoulder and faced the group again. Yogianni receded into the corner and watched with the feigned interest of a magician's assistant.

"Look into your partner's eyes. Don't stare, just look. Make your eyes soft. Try to connect with your partner."

Paula gazed into this stranger's eyes.

"Some of you have stopped breathing," Sky Spacious instructed. "Keep breathing! Feel your nose hairs. It's a trip — a pleasure palace of self-soothing."

Paula *was* breathing and looking into the stranger's eyes. This was more difficult than she had thought. If she looked she stopped breathing; if she breathed, she stopped looking.

What she saw were hard dark eyes that looked too frightened to even notice her. He was holding his breath. No, it couldn't be fear, she thought. He's a grown man. But yes, it was fear.

"Just breathe and stop your inner dialogues." It was Sky Spacious again. If Paula stopped her inner dialogue, she forgot to breathe. If she heard her inner dialogue, she breathed but stopped looking into her partner's eyes. It seemed complicated. She couldn't even feel her nose hairs.

She heard grunts and giggles from somewhere deep in the room. She glanced over to see if Ralph was having an easier time but still couldn't find him. He had the nerve to be laughing and giggling with his partner after all the grief he had given her in the garden!

She was panicked and angry, but realized that she had to keep these feelings under wraps for the time being.

"Let's not talk, but check into your own unique being and see what you are feeling right at this moment," Sky Spacious instructed.

Paula realized that she had been holding her breath, too. She wanted to be a good student. She had always been the most obedient and quickest student in the class.

She wondered what her eyes communicated to this guy, so she put a smile on her face, so he would know that she was friendly.

Then it occurred to her that she didn't really know a soul in the room but her husband. Another panic wave went through her. She wondered who all these other people really were in the room. Some of them wore very loose-fitting sarongs. Their prints reminded Paula of colors she saw behind her closed eyelids after coming in from bright sunlight — puce, fuchsia, day-glow orange and aqua. Paula was decked out in her Nordstrom cruise wear. They all had to leave their shoes at the door upon arrival. It didn't look like anyone else wore Arche sandals. Her dad had said that you could always tell a person by her shoes. She felt terribly overdressed, as if she were back at fourth grade in a new school.

If the exercises called for Ralph to go off with his partner, she would be very alone and lost with this stranger in front of her. He showed no interest in her whatsoever. She felt invisible.

Her eyes shot around the dim room. Everyone seemed to be enjoying themselves. They were breathing and looking into each other's eyes for what seemed to be forever.

Finally, Yogianni said, "Time's up. Let's sit down on the floor or find a pillow, and talk to your partner about this experience for ten minutes. Take turns. Don't hog the conversation."

A little giggle filled the room as people recognized their natural tendencies.

She didn't even know this guy's name. "Hi, I'm Paula," she said to break the ice. Her mom always taught her that men needed to be "drawn out." She could ask him what he did for a living. Then he would reciprocate with the same question. She wanted him to ask her what she did for a living. It always made her feel so important, and she did command a lot of respect from her work identity. It was as if she would be nothing without her business card. But she was conflicted because then, everyone would come flocking to her with photos of who they were in the sixties and name-drop as to who they knew. It had happened time and time again in her travels, although it didn't seem to happen just a half an hour ago at dinner. She hated to discuss business when her meter wasn't running.

"I'm Duke." Then she saw him shift his eyes off her and scan the room, probably looking for his blonde bombshell. She took this opportunity to scout for her husband, but she still didn't see Ralph anywhere.

Paula felt a pang of rejection from her new partner. After all, she had invested time in looking into the eyes of this guy, and he didn't seem interested in even carrying on a polite conversation or following directions. Why had she come?

"Are you married to her?" Paula asked, looking in the same direction his eyes were stationed, trying to draw him back into the conversation. She didn't want him to think that she was judgmental or unattractive in any way. She would try harder, that's all.

"Delila, no. I've been divorced twice. I just sold my restaurant in Steamboat and I'm living out here now. I met Delila in a workshop. Actually, she was the speaker. She's a *real* workshop leader too, in Marin County, California. We've been together for about four months."

He nodded in the direction of where Delila was last seen, but she had disappeared again. Paula put on her best smile. Duke was preoccupied, that was clear.

"How come you are here?"

"Delila thought we needed it. She's into things like this. She is a dance therapist and leads transformational groups, and wants me to get some training so we can lead groups together."

"I guess we're supposed to talk about what we experienced just now," said Paula, trying to create some conversation and take their minds off their partners. "When I looked into your eyes, they were very hazel." Yogianni hadn't told them to stop gazing yet.

"So are yours," Duke replied mechanically.

Fortunately, Sky Spacious stepped in.

"Time out. I want you all to go back to your partners and share the experience of how that felt."

Paula breathed a sigh of relief. She wouldn't have to invent something else to say to Duke.

Yogianni stepped in front of Sky and smiled, one of those confident group-leader smiles. She waved her arms, ushering her minions back to find the partners they came with.

Paula spotted Ralph after several seconds, shuffling his legs and with some difficulty trying to get out of his crossed-legged seated position. She rushed across the room. Other couples were finding one another and going off together in hushed serious whispers.

When Paula finally got to Ralph's side, she said sarcastically, "Boy, she sure *grabbed* you!"

"She *was* intense."

"What was that like for you?" What Paula really meant was, did you like her?

"Well, it was very strange staring into someone's eyes that I hardly knew."

Paula breathed a sigh of relief. "Me too. He was hunting for his partner the whole time. He was so frightened that he wouldn't get her back! Why did you pick her?"

"Honey, you saw what happened, I didn't pick her, she jumped on me before I could even look around the room and choose. She's spinning like a top. She couldn't stop gabbing the whole time we were together."

Paula knew Ralph hated women who were non-stop talkers, so this quelled her anxiety considerably.

Before Ralph had a chance to share any more with Paula, Sky was calling the group back together up at the front of the room and trying to get their attention by waving his dashiki-covered arms.

"We have a lot to discuss and not much time. I want to demonstrate the next step in contact," Sky said. "When you go back to your rooms tonight, and every night you are here, you will have homework, and not the kind that you got at school, but wish you had." Someone giggled faintly.

"You had a taste of making contact with an attractive stranger and it must have called up many feelings. Tonight in your rooms, I want you to make intimate contact with your partner through sustained eye contact. It will feel different because it is a private space and you have a history with your partner that you didn't have with the person you chose or who chose you here." His eyes took in the whole group before he continued.

"So now that you will practice that, we will go to the next step. My lovely Tantriki, Yogianni, the Goddess of Tortola, and I will give you a demonstration in finding your beloved G spot."

With the flair of someone who had done this many times before, Yogianni carefully dragged a mattress from the corner of the room and positioned it in the middle of the wood floor. Then she spread out a lavender sheet and a lacy mauve silk shawl with fringes on top of the sheet. She slipped out of her see-through scarves and lay on her back with her head facing Sky, ready for his instructions.

Yogianni lay buck-naked in front of the room, gazing invitingly into Sky's eyes. Her breasts were like two firm scoops of ice cream riding the raft of her ribs. Sky gave a running commentary, as if he were hosting a Saturday afternoon football game, while he took off his shirt and with one motion bolted out of his pants.

Her hair had become more chaotic since the beginning of the session. The loose tendrils had graduated to hanks, and where it was meant to be smooth and pulled back, tiny, fuzzy sprigs had reared up, creating a sort of corona around her scalp.

Paula was amazed at Sky's speed. He reminded her of some type of animal, a goat, perhaps. It was those eyes: almost slit-shaped pupils, and dark. She wondered what it was like to be married to a man like Sky. He was so sexy and seemed so at home with lovemaking, yet he was so frighteningly sensual.

Yogianni remained silent, smiling provocatively like Vanna White on *Wheel of Fortune*, waiting for direction on which numbers to expose.

Sky put his hand deep inside Yogianni's vagina as the group watched. It seemed to Paula that it was much like gutting a chicken. "You see, women have this fluid called Amrita, which flows out in profusion when you find the G spot and you rub it."

He stepped up the action with his hand. It looked like his whole arm was deep inside her by this time.

Yogianni appeared to be a very thin woman, Paula saw. Her body seemed to fold in half at the waist like a piece of paper. Paula was transfixed, and then she quietly slipped toward the front of the room to get a better view. Ralph followed.

"It is very satisfying to a woman. It feels like coming home to them." Sky looked around the room. Yogianni nodded up at Sky, not losing her eye contact.

"Most women love this, but they themselves can't seem to tell you where it is, because they haven't explored their body, due to all the years of early childhood shame about sex."

By this time, Yogianni was writhing with pleasure. Soon a clear gooey liquid was spurting out of her.

Paula, Ralph, Duke, Delila, Reefdancer and Miracle, Antonio and his two women were mesmerized. Everyone was transfixed. It wasn't clear whether Yogianni was having an orgasm, really, or just writhing with pleasure and spurting clear liquid like a lava flow.

Paula wondered where *her* G spot was and why Ralph had never found it for her!

Sky continued to demonstrate, to Yogianni's pleasure. Paula noted that in the supine position Yogianni appeared to be a little older than she had first thought. She could tell by the lighting and the way Yogianni's skin seemed to be pulled down by the weight of gravity. This alone made Paula feel a bit more comfortable. If Yogianni could find her G spot, Paula was determined that with Ralph's help, she would find her own. Maybe this was the path to happiness after all.

Ralph watched with curiosity and cynicism. He was beginning to get a migraine on the left side of his eye. The evening had been too intense. He remembered that he would have to endure it because he had left his aspirin kit in the room on the bed.

There was something about this act and this woman that rang very phony to Ralph. He didn't know why. He wondered if she was having a real orgasm or a made-for-television orgasm. Was she having one at all? If he was going to have to find Paula's G spot that night, would Paula ask him, or would she wait to see if he asked her, and if he didn't, would she start an argument? He decided that he would have to go for broke and suggest it himself. It wasn't that he was adverse to this kind of archeological dig, it's just that it looked sort of messy and it took time. He hoped that his migraine would go away and his mosquito bites would stop itching so he could please Paula. He just didn't want to have to work too hard to find this G spot. She wouldn't understand, of course, because she could be quite demanding, and this activity-oriented sexual exploration was a whole new thing. Besides it didn't seem to help Sky get excited or get off. It seemed like it was all for Yogianni's pleasure. What kind of sex was that? That was a massage, Ralph decided. You pay people to do that, well, not *that*. He hoped that his migraine wouldn't interfere. It was one thing for a woman to claim a migraine to avoid sex, another entirely for a man.

Ralph looked around the room. He was feeling queasy with this graphic performance, but it seemed like everyone else was in awe or shock at such a private act.

"I'll show you where mine is, in the room," Paula whispered mischievously.

Now Ralph knew he was going to have to rise to the occasion, or disappoint Paula.

After the demonstration, Yogianni passed around a sheet to sign up for coaching in each couple's room. It cost $250 an hour. Paula was the first name on the list. She knew it would be well worth it. She had never been observed, much less coached by a third person, in the act of making love.

She looked around the now dim room. Ralph had left her side. She couldn't find Ralph or Delila.

Yogianni, several yards away, wondered if Ralph was turned on by her work that evening. Out of all the guys she knew there, and all the new ones, he seemed like some real talent she wanted to explore. She wondered how serious he was with his partner. Near the door that night Paula was determined to pursue the quest for the G spot. Little did she know that she would be getting much more Amrita than she bargained for.

12

Paula walked out into the dark night alone. She could feel the balmy night air soaking into the sun-besotted shores of Tortola. The lei of clouds that lay upon the rolling green flanks of Sage Mountain gave way to a crystal clear starry night. The air was bursting with smells of eucalypti, bananas, and the sweet smell of frangipani and sage. It reminded her of their home in Mill Valley.

Some of the group filtered out from the workshop, sipping from large mugs of immune support tea, others poked around on the deck looking at the expanse of the Caribbean below.

Paula couldn't understand why Delila had rushed toward Ralph. Was her husband so desirable, and she alone couldn't see it? And where was he now? Paula was getting that awful feeling in her stomach. Things weren't going right.

Out stepped Yogianni from the darkness. The night air caught the hem of her charmeuse skirt, lifting it, while she negotiated the deck like a ballerina, long, lithe, and about five years younger than Paula, who felt a pang of envy at her youth and energy. Paula had been wrong inside when she assessed Yogianni's age.

"I saw you signed up for some Tantric coaching tonight. Where is your partner?" Yogianni said.

"He's my husband. I don't know where he is at the moment." Paula was feeling a little defensive with a missing husband afoot. She supposed that after an evening of instruction like this, she should be in a romantic embrace with Ralph. Instead she was alone. Paula caught the guardedness in her voice and softened it a little.

"Well, let me know when I can come up, okay?" Yogianni acted somewhat indifferent, like it was a job that she did every day of the week, and nothing more. She was just being responsible in carrying it out. At least on the surface, it appeared that way to Paula.

Nonetheless, Yogianni had been observing Ralph all evening, and there was a certain indefinable something about him that attracted her. Was it how he carried his six foot-plus frame, his confidence about himself as he talked? She noticed that he was the first to be chosen, and she was slightly interested. She thought that if she had an opportunity, and if she could make Sky jealous, he might be more inclined to deal with her needs. Sure, Ralph probably couldn't compete with Sky in the sexual arena, but he had a certain power about him that was altogether different than Sky, and she was curious as to what that was.

"Yes, come up tonight about eight." Paula tried to remain in control, but of course, she knew that she was losing control. Things were happening too fast and she couldn't process it all.

Not far away, Ralph had lost control moments ago. Losing control was something Ralph was pretty unfamiliar with. Paula had accused him often that control was really his middle name. Every fork and spoon had to be lined up in its little slot in the silverware drawer. He told their cleaning lady not to touch his study.

In fact, the idea of dumping Ralph was seeping back into Paula's consciousness at that moment. In her meditation class back in Marin, they had discussed one of the five precepts. It was about not killing another living thing. Paula had blurted out, "Kill with a capital K, or a small K? Does that mean you couldn't kill a husband, but you could kill a spider?" Her Zen teacher, a self declared eco-vegan-feminist named Padma, responded, "I guess it depends on how many legs it has."

Without Ralph in her life, she would be free. She could get another animal. Yes, she'd probably get some kittens. She already had two old cats, but Ralph said that if she brought home any more cats, they could sleep on his side of the bed. He'd be gone. She had a sneaking suspicion that without Ralph, she would become one of those women over fifty she often spied at cat shows. They were alone, "had let themselves go," a term her mother used, and were all decked out in cat paraphernalia: the cat sweatshirt with little rhinestones for the cat's eyes, winged and glitter-framed cat sunglasses, the baseball cap with little cat ears on the sides. And of course, the dangling cat earrings.

She immediately used what she had learned in her seminar on Transformation Thought Breakthroughs to stifle that thought. Instead, she went in search of her husband.

Ralph was sitting in the dark with Delila. He was wondering why this strange woman smelled so good. He closed his eyes and breathed in deeply, trying to locate that odor somewhere in his primal male brain. Suddenly he got it. She smelled a little like Jo Jo Beads, a candy Ralph loved to eat at the Saturday matinees when he was a kid. He took another deep breath and smiled softly to himself. He was beginning to become attracted to Delila. This attraction was a new feeling for him. It started in his loins and moved up his belly. He hadn't felt this way for a woman in a long time. It felt new and strange and wonderful.

In that moment, he was glad he had come after all. Yet, there was another part of him that was spiteful and wanted to show Paula that he couldn't be controlled or duped, so he lingered longer with Delila than he knew he should.

Delila pulled a little zip-lock bag out of her purse, opened it, and handed some of the contents to Ralph.

"What's that?"

"Oh, just some dope brownies I baked up, here, take some."

Ralph dug around in the bag and gulped down two brownies.

"You better watch it," Delila said, turning toward Ralph, "eat them *slooowly*. I must have dumped about a pound of marijuana into these things." She laughed and grabbed Ralph's hand to slow him down.

"Where did you get this stuff?"

"I got it from Reefdancer. He and some friends came here in the 'sixties, dropped off the grid and started growing this stuff. Good, huh?"

"Oh, so these guys are *all* dope dealers?" Ralph asked incredulously. He had never been in the company of such nefarious characters before. In the corporate world they remained well disguised. The only guilty pleasures he and Paula indulged in were Häagen-Dazs ice cream in bed with a good video. He wouldn't even know who his local drug dealer was in Marin.

"No, just a few are *farmers* here on the island!" Delila laughed. "In fact, Reefdancer and Miracle just 'smoked' a dear friend that died recently."

"What?"

"Well, we had cremated Georgianne and we got some of her ashes, so we sprinkled them in a joint that we shared, and smoked Georgianne. Cool, huh?"

Ralph didn't grasp it, and didn't know what he thought of that activity, because his mind was slowing down.

"Can I think about that and get back to you about it later?"

Delila smiled pleasantly at him.

"Don't the authorities come by and bust them?" The brownies were affecting him.

"Nope."

Some other people from the workshop came drifting over and Delila offered each a brownie. They gathered in a small circle around Ralph and Delila.

Ralph was admiring the colors of Delila's fringed shawl and how they blended in with the cerulean blue-green of her eyes.

About that moment, several hundred yards away, Paula was talking to Reefdancer. She had forgotten momentarily about Ralph, and was deeply engaged in conversation. *He looks like Tom Cruise*, Paula thought.

He was telling her about his ranch with twenty-five horses, and four dogs and two cats that ran free, when they turned the corner and spied Delila and Ralph talking and laughing, surrounded by the others. Delila beckoned to them.

"Have some brownies." Delila lifted the bag to offer the pair some food. She was now the center of attraction as she pulled out another even bigger zip-lock bag.

"Boy, you came prepared," Reefdancer said. He grabbed a brownie and handed one to Paula. Paula bit into it and commented on Delila's culinary abilities. It just hit the spot for dessert this time of night. It tasted sweet, soft and chocolatey.

Paula looked over at Ralph. He held a brownie toward her in a gesture of making a toast. Paula felt her insides calm down a little. At least she knew where he was now, but she still felt like things were moving a little too fast for her taste.

Paula sensed her brain chemistry changing quickly from the ingredients inside the brownies. She saw herself staring into Tom Cruise's eyes, she heard herself talk, she stood outside herself and saw herself listening to him talk about breaking in a pony he just bought.

Paula never had ridden a horse. In fact, the closest she had ever gotten to one was watching *Gunsmoke* on television when she was a kid. She had fallen in love with James Arness and used him unconsciously as a role model for the kind of men she was attracted to. She realized that she had no idea what Reefdancer was talking about, but his eyes were so deep and mysterious, she kept hers glued to them. Maybe this was what Sky Spacious had been talking about earlier. She couldn't tell the difference between horses and horsemeat. This gorgeous man didn't know that she was a girl raised in Manhattan, who thought peas came from the frozen food compartment of Gristedes Market. Before she came to California she thought that palm trees were made of plastic. The only palm she had ever seen was outside Robert Hall's men's clothing store in Newark.

But Ralph was noticing. Sitting within yards of his wife, he began feeling an emotion he hated. Jealousy filled him. In Paula and Ralph's world in Marin, they never had time to slow down and smoke some grass. Their world was filled with earning potential, career advancement and the latest new possession. At dinner parties you impressed your friends with your newest computer, how far up the mountain you lived, if your house was paid-off or not, and did you rent or own. Or you showed them your new day timer or dropped the name of a movie star who just became your new neighbor. It was a whole different scene. If you did drugs, it was cocaine, but they didn't hang out with those coke people. They just read about them getting busted in the news.

Ralph grabbed some more brownies because it seemed like everyone was having fun but him. Delila had left the brownie bag open for any takers and had sidled back to Duke, laughing and snuggling into him near the railing of the deck. She wanted to make sure everyone knew he was taken. She threw her head back and tossed her long, thick, blonde hair.

Suddenly this situation didn't make any sense to Ralph. Ralph and Paula had been married longer than dirt, but a weird churning in his intestines began taking hold of him. He couldn't continue thinking through the developing blue haze. He saw Paula's glassy eyes staring at this strange dude, their meaningful smiles, and how the dude reached out and brushed a strand of hair off her forehead. What was Paula doing right in front of him, gazing into another man's eyes with a look of love?

"Oh my gawd," Ralph moaned and then gave a hysterical cry. "I think I'm dying!" Suddenly he launched his two hundred-twenty pound, six-foot-two frame off the bench and fell with a loud thud.

Everyone turned to look at him. He landed sprawled out on the redwood deck. He lay there moaning, as one by one, the Tantric group moved closely in around him to observe with a drugged curiosity. Reefdancer leaned over Ralph, put his face down on Ralph's chest to listen to his heart, and then twisted his neck upward to face the crowd.

"Bumm-ummer, looks like this guy is in serious trouble, maybe a heart attack," he said in a concerned voice.

Paula rushed to Ralph's side. Was this for real or a false alarm? After years of Ralph's dramatic moments, Paula was embarrassed. She leaned over his body and whispered into his ear. "Ralph, just try to pretend that you're normal." She found that sometimes he wore a band-aid just in case he needed one. *What kind of impression must we be making?* she thought. She was torn between her loyalty to Ralph and her irritation that he was making such a scene. The bug-eyed, stoned-to-the-gills participants leaned over him to get a better look.

"Oh-God-help-shit-help," she prayed. Where was her God now? Where was her Charlton Heston look-alike? Where was that tall man with a flowing white beard, soft blue eyes, wearing a cotton robe and holding a staff?

"Give the guy air, give him air," shouted Reefdancer, pushing people back.

Paula knew that Jewish men seemed to be missing a gene in one department — the stoic gene. Having been married twice before, and both to non-Jewish men, she knew that Christian men met illness with quiet forbearance. Jewish men like Ralph, on the other hand, and her girlfriends' Jewish husbands, had two missing genes. Jewish men may be better lovers and more sensitive, but it was a tradeoff because they were hypochondriacs when it came to cut fingers, pimples suddenly appearing on their face, a cough or even the flu. They had to be babied and coddled. They made you give them the cough medicine on a clean spoon from the kitchen, whereas her other husbands just chug-a-lugged the syrup like real men.

The second missing gene was in the home improvement department. Ralph thought the circuit breaker was a word used to describe an Olympic runner when he came around the track to the finish line.

She remembered how they had fought in the garden about staying, and his complaint about getting a virus from the mosquitoes. Just last week, they were at a friend's barbeque where Ralph was bitten by a mosquito, and he got hysterical about coming down with flu. He was so suggestible that sometimes he could talk to someone he didn't like and come down with the flu moments later. She was skeptical this time, but she wasn't going to dismiss his collapse outright quite yet.

She knelt down and looked into his sweating, cold face. "Honey, what is it? Where does it hurt?" She was still seeing his face swimming before her as she felt her own brain cells expanding and contracting in her head. "Is it your heart?"

"It feels like I'm having an appendicitis attack," he moaned.

Paula knew Ralph had had his appendix out when he was a kid. She wondered if perhaps it had grown back.

"My heart, my heart," he moaned

"Where?" Paula was feeling his chest.

"I feel shooting pains in my heart."

"Get a doctor! Get a doctor! Is there a doctor nearby?" Paula shouted.

Antonio had just rushed off to get his acupuncturist in town when Miracle came up the path. She had been working giving colonics all day long down the road at the Paradise Health Retreat and Garden Spa. She moved her hefty frame fluidly through the crowd and stood over Ralph. Reefdancer reached up to take her hand and spoke to her first.

"Honey, this guy is in trouble, can we use your car and go get a doctor?" He gave her a hug and put his arm around her.

She bent down and spoke to Ralph. "Where is the pain?"

Ralph just moaned at first, and then he volunteered, "In my belly and shooting into my heart."

Miracle settled herself next to him and began rubbing his stomach clockwise as she cooed to him softly. She was very gentle, soft and voluptuous in her approach. Paula hated her for touching her husband.

As Miracle rubbed, Paula launched into her own silent patchwork prayer. "Oh-God-Oh-Shit-Oh-God-Help!" She felt like a spiritual outsider, on the other side of Christianity's velvet rope, unable to enter the club because some beefy bouncer at the door insisted that she didn't have the right credentials.

"What did you eat today, honey?" Miracle kept rubbing and talking.

Ralph silently extended his arm and lifted up an empty bag of dope brownies, as little brown crumbs scattered around his head.

Miracle laughed and kept touching his stomach while everyone watched sympathetically.

What happened next defied interpretation. Ralph let out a cry and went running to the bathroom.

The group waited like silent zombies, listening to the moaning reach great proportions inside.

"Call an ambulance!" Reefdancer cried. Miracle raised her hand and stopped him with a silent gesture. She sat on the deck where Ralph had been and smiled enigmatically.

Several minutes later, Ralph emerged from the bathroom with a silly smirk on his face. He turned toward Miracle, and then the group.

"I guess I ate too many brownies. That sure relieved the pressure," he said extending his arm toward the bathroom. "It must have been gas." They heard the bowl flushing.

He lifted Miracle in his arms and gave her a hug, then turned toward the group.

"Thanks, you guys, you saved my life."

13

That night, Ralph and Paula were buried cozily under the comforter in their cabin. They heard the tropical rain and wind howl outside. It intensified the fragrances of midnight jasmine and pikaki through their open window. Then night rain calmed to a soft and balmy drizzle.

She often thought of Ralph and herself as Hansel and Gretel, lost and trying to find their way. She thought of herself as the cleverer of the two, because she would be the one to plan ahead and drop the bread along the path. But then it occurred to her that in the fairy tale, the birds ate up the bread trail and they stumbled into the wicked witch. She dropped that analogy and looked over at Ralph. She mused that he, like most men, appeared more physically at home in the world, while she was more emotionally at home.

However, once again, the events of the day did not bear that out at all. She was more confused than ever about her relationship with Ralph. Today she had discovered that there were some luscious men out there, but then again, there were some women who found Ralph very attractive and they were not very subtle about it, either.

She pondered. Ralph and she were like old houses when they first met. Fixer-upper projects. They had done a lot for each other's confidence and ambition over the years. They had been together a long time, like an old investment, and she was going to be really careful about letting it go, at least for now. She saw the way these new-age women hovered over him, especially Delila and Yogianni, while Ralph acted like a little lost sheep. Women just loved little improvement projects, men who represented the possibility of being open to changing themselves for their benefit as a show of love.

The knock on the door stopped her mental meandering in midstream. There stood Yogianni in a rain-drenched coat.

"Remember, you signed up for my sexual assistance tonight," she said somewhat tersely as she stepped into the room uninvited.

Paula was caught off-guard. Ralph awoke from his nap and looked up with an inquisitive expression.

"It has been a hard day for Ralph, and we really haven't had a chance to discuss this together, and . . ." Paula knew she had really messed up this time. She hadn't consulted Ralph at all.

"What is she going to do?"

"I took the liberty of signing us up." Paula was remembering the conversation about her style of pushing and not asking on the ride up to the workshop. "Actually I paid for this." Paula thought that if she said that she spent money already, Ralph would go for it. "She's going to help us with our lovemaking,"

"Two women?" Ralph asked incredulously. He hadn't forgotten his attraction to Delila that afternoon. Suddenly he forgot about his migraine and the mosquito bites because this workshop was getting better and better. "Well, let's get going."

Paula was surprised at his response, but before she could protest, Yogianni took off her coat and draped it over a chair near the door. She knew what hard work these older couples could be, and she had even taken a nap after the workshop, so she would be in good shape. She could tell that they were in some one-note-Charlie rut with their sex life, and she was determined to change that. Sky Spacious hadn't certified her for nothing. At least she had a certification in something, she thought. Ralph was attractive. There was an unpredictability about him, despite his put-on goofy manner. She wasn't sure about Paula; she was a wild card.

"So what I'm going to do, is to get you both comfortable, and then I will facilitate you so Paula can achieve multiple orgasms. How is your sex life now, any problems?"

Stupidly, Paula looked at Ralph and then at Yogianni. It hardly occurred to her that this was a strange question. A woman she doesn't know walks in out of the rain and asks her about her sex life, but the promise of multiple orgasms was blurring her thinking.

"We are doing okay," Paula said defensively, looking at Ralph, "we just need some sprucing up."

Yogianni led Paula into the bathroom. "You go take a shower and get yourself nice and clean, put on something soft and sexy, and come back out. I'll get Ralph ready."

After the door to the bathroom was closed, Yogianni turned around and faced Ralph alone for the first time. She assessed the situation with her she-instincts. He was definitely filled with repressed pheromones that she must release. It was a shame she had to release them with his wife. Maybe there would be something extra left for her.

She opened a satchel she had brought and reached in.

A familiar fragrance of sandalwood emerged from the mysterious leather insides. It did not go unnoticed by Ralph. He saw a tattoo of a leopard on her right thigh. This aroused him. "My sexual assistant tools," she smiled when she saw Ralph

117

lean over the bed and peer into the bag. Out of the satchel, she pulled a short gauzy kimono and then she stepped out of her camisole, DKNY thong underpants, and slipped into the see-through flowered wrap. All of this was well-rehearsed from her certification training.

Ralph's synapses and dendrites short-circuited. His primal brain didn't know whom he should be attracted to. Yogianni looked delicious, but then Paula stepped out of the bathroom at that moment in a little camisole and nothing else. On her feet she wore Ralph's favorite red plastic stiletto heels. He felt himself go hard.

Paula instinctively knew she had to one-up Yogianni. Her intuition told her that men imprinted from an early age by leafing through the pages of *Playboy* and *Hustler*. She often teased Ralph that just waving a garter belt in front of his face could cause his erection. She knew the red heels were key here. He would fixate on them and not Yogianni, of whom she was now wary.

Yogianni eased onto the bed, but kept her two feet on the floor. She felt Ralph's attraction to her, but she didn't want to threaten Paula or appear too forward and spook the couple. She knew how to bide her time. After all, this was a work gig, she reminded herself.

Once Paula and Ralph were settled in the bed, Yogianni began her lesson.

"Ralph, I want you to find Paula's G spot, just like you saw in class. I want you to put your index and middle finger inside and circle around her vagina and explore. Together you will find the landmarks of pleasure, the Black Pearl of Joy."

Sky Spacious had taught her to talk in metaphors. Couples like that, he said, It was classier.

In Yogianni's coat pocket she carried three business cards: one as a real estate agent for ABC Oceanside Realty, one as a housecleaner for Caribbean Mer-Maids, and one for Sky Spacious' group. That one read: Yogianni, senior Tantriki goddess. It was like Cher or Charo or Garbo: one name. One name defined her. She liked that.

She actually liked that card the best because that's where she made the most money. If her Midwestern mother could see her now, she would surely die, Yogianni thought briefly as she got more deeply into her goddess role.

It took a while to be trained by Sky. He may not have been that attractive to her, but he sure had an ace in his hand. He knew more than any man she ever met about how to create excruciating pleasure for women of all ages. Once, when he was on his boat and was sitting across from her, after a few drinks he took his big toe and found her crotch. In front of everyone he nuzzled his way into her bikini bottom and stuck his big toe into her warm soft spot. While he did this, he lectured the group on the G spot, his favorite topic. She went wild with joy. Before she met Sky, she had Obsessive Compulsive Disorder in politeness. She would even call back telephone solicitors. But she and other women couldn't stay away from Sky. After Sky, she got over her politeness. Sky loved to pleasure women. What could she do anyway? She wasn't about to leave when she got such attention as his wife and star in all his workshops. But Sky really held the key to pleasure and he knew it.

"I'm like bees are to honey," he would say to her privately after a long, hot tropical afternoon of making love around his pool.

After all this time, all Yogianni could figure out was that Sky only wanted sex and more sex with a variety of women. Even at his age, when other men were winding down, he seemed insatiable. She couldn't understand it.

For Yogianni, this work was better than housecleaning, although in that line of work, she could look through people's stuff in private.

Speaking of private, Yogianni rested her eyes on Ralph's risen male part. She didn't remember the last time she had seen such a big one. Some women have all the luck.

Yogianni noticed Paula's feet. Those heels are something! We gotta do something about her "get up." Nineteen sixty-five must have been a banner year for this woman. Yogianni made a mental note to say something to Paula about her outfit, after she had built some bedside rapport and trust with the couple.

Ralph's primal brain continued to short circuit as he grabbed Paula and mounted her. Paula looked towards Yogianni with confusion in her eyes.

Are we paying Yogianni mega-bucks to be a spectator to our meat and potatoes lovemaking? Paula wondered.

Without a moment's hesitation, Yogianni, professional that she was, grabbed Ralph by the scruff of the neck, like a garden variety alley cat, and shouted up against his face,

"Not so fast, big brother."

Ralph rolled off Paula with a reddened face and his primal brain just fizzled as the two women watched.

"That isn't the way it works, Big Boy. You must pleasure the woman first," Yogianni insisted.

Ralph, always a consummate learner and figuring that they were paying Yogianni big money, decided at that moment that he better get his money's worth. Whatever that meant.

Yogianni looked over at Paula and asked, "May I show him?"

Sky had taught them to always get the wife's permission first. Paula nodded in consent. What else could she do in the heat of the moment?

Then Yogianni mounted the fizzled member and showed Ralph with her wet index finger where his fingers should be inserted.

"This is the G spot, and go a little closer to the opening and you will find the A spot, the B spot and the C spot."

Paula, always priding herself on being the good student, watched attentively. Although still wary and feeling competitive, it felt kind of sexy watching another woman make love to her husband. It gave her a new perspective, like seeing someone test-drive your new car.

Ralph was really getting off on all the feminine attention and in no time he got the hang of this Tantric sex thing.

For several long hours he pleasured Paula and Yogianni with his fingers and his mouth. Finally, Yogianni gave him the okay to insert his primal brain into Paula's warm soft spot. From Paula's moans and Ralph's grunts, she could tell that it had never been better for either of them in all their years of marriage.

Paula felt proud of Ralph and his new-found talents. She felt differently about him after that night.

About midnight, Yogianni slid her coat off the chair. It was dry by now in the steamy room. She slipped outside, leaving her two cherubs asleep in each other's arms. She knew she had done well, and she vowed to play Ralph's instrument again before the weekend was out, regardless of how Paula might feel.

14

Duke hadn't meant to do anything untoward. He was intent on scouring down the rented kayaks with pails of water and detergent, then hoisting them atop the large iron racks on the roof of his SUV.

As he was doing this he was thinking that if he could amass enough money, he would own these kayaks someday. He hoped to be the biggest outfitter on this end of the island.

This part of the island was remote and rocky terrain, seaweed-covered. The noise of percussive sea vibrated under the jagged rocks. Few lived here. Of course, there were man-made paths over the jagged rocks to little inlets and tide pools where locals could swim in the clear aquamarine waters or fish for parrot fish, Christmas wrasse, hebi or groupie. Coral in shades of yellow and mauves reflected up through the floor of the pools.

If he were stranded, he knew he couldn't starve on this end of the island. But at this time of night all the tourists had gone back to their hotels to take a hot shower and get ready for dinner. Perhaps they would have a drink on their balconies and watch the sunset, and he was left here alone to see the big red glow disappear over the horizon. He was savoring this solitude as he counted the money he had made that day. Mostly ones and tens filled his wallet on this trip. This was a hell of a way to make a living, but it was always a trade-off for him. He wasn't afraid of working hard. His clients were often fat people who didn't know how to swim, spoiled kids, and Midwestern-ers from Chicago fleeing from the snow. He was happy because the work afforded him the freedom he needed. It was outdoors and he was his own man. Sometimes he hated the rich bitches who hired him, but he chose this life and was trying to make a go of it with Delila.

It was so still here. He focused on the sounds of the lapping of the surf and the shifting of the stones rolling back into the vast ocean. This was a desolate locale this time of night, and that's why he was surprised to hear a rustling in the bushes. Duke wasn't the kind of guy to be afraid of anything in the physical world that he wouldn't consider exciting or a challenge. It was the emotional world that most confounded him. He couldn't understand Delila's moods. He was noticing lately, as he got to know her better, that she frequently made a study of grinding her ax of self-esteem on him. Offer her a fine piece of jewelry, and she would say, "Oh, my old lover shopped at Tiffany's." In the feeling arena, he felt remedial compared to her self-expressiveness. She always knew what she was feeling, instantaneously. In contrast, he felt like a vast wasteland of feelings from his neck down. He tried to keep that hidden for fear that if his woman found out she would discard him, like so many had.

He walked toward the thorn trees that grew out of the rock outcropping. He was surprised to see a slender woman of indiscernible age, perhaps crowding fifty. Time had seized upon her eye sockets and the seams around her mouth and nose. And at that moment, out of her nose came a loud, long, high wheezing. She was sleeping and snoring very loudly.

His glance took in the surroundings. She had made a lean-to supported by branches and twigs with a pareo from cotton material. It served as a covering for a roof. *She must be living here*, he thought. He had run across other marginal people finding shelters on the island to live in, subsisting in gullies and sand dunes, but never a woman. Mostly they were guys his age, old surfer bums left from the 'sixties who couldn't find work, or men on the lam. He had stumbled across druggies on the slide down, and young beach bums who took pride in not being on any voter registration and never having paid taxes. Sometimes, he'd see Vietnam vets who were a little off who believed that the Vietnam war was still raging. Maybe the heat and humidity caused them to lose some of their marbles. He stood there pondering for several minutes, just taking in this peculiar scene.

He saw that her struggles were stamped on the wildness of wrinkles in her tanned and taut skin. Yet, there was nostalgia in her appearance, some charming feminine sense of the past, like an old-fashioned Christmas card.

Maybe she could feel his presence, or his shadow crossed her face for a second, creating a momentary coolness; startled, she woke up.

She talked like a little girl in a tiny, whispery voice, separating one word from another. "Who are you?" she stammered, rubbing her eyes and seeming to move from the innocence of sleep to the consciousness that a stranger was gazing upon her. Her hair was shoulder-length and straw-like. Her bloom was fading.

He noticed that she had almost perfect teeth except for an empty space where one of her front teeth should be. He pointed. "What happened to your tooth?" Hardly a way to begin a conversation.

"It got knocked out in a fight awhile ago." She smiled tentatively at him.

"What's your name?"

"Fawn."

"I'm Duke."

"Oh."

"You live here?"

"Yeah, right here." She paused. "For now."

He saw a metal shopping cart filled with belongings wedged into the rocks. Atop the cart was a live rooster standing stock still, like a cardboard cut-out, and staring with piercing eyes right through him.

"Who's that? Your dinner?" laughed Duke. By this time, he felt like he had entered some other reality. He knew that he couldn't linger because he had to pack up and get the kayaks back to the rental place before they closed.

"Oh, that's Rudolph, my companion." She had the most unusual smile. It was a cross between sheer innocence and the craziness of a demented old woman.

"Not dinner?"

"No, I don't usually eat dinner, and especially not my watch rooster."

"Oh, like a watch dog?"

"Correct."

Duke sensed that he was talking to a waif. Her clothes were thin and frayed, like those of someone who was down on her luck. She seemed to be one of those women who cling to the mannerisms and graces of a small child. He felt awful leaving her there, and besides, she might be hungry.

"I have some protein bars in the truck."

"That'll do, I've had worse."

"No, let me pack up and take you someplace for a quick dinner. Then if you want, I can drop you back here."

Why would a guy who has a job and probably a girl do that, if not for a kind heart? she thought.

She helped him load the truck, but he could tell that she barely had any strength. It was as if the sun had leached out all her physical energy.

"You are so thin, don't you eat?"

They were driving along the dirt road leading to the strip mall and Road Town Deli. Duke knew he couldn't be too late because Delila was waiting, surely wondering where he was. She probably had dinner in the oven warming for him, but his heart was pounding with compassion for this woman's plight.

As he gulped down a certified Range Free Angus Burger and organic fries, and she picked at her food, she described herself and her circumstances unhesitatingly. He discovered that she had lived on the island before, and after some downturn on her luck on the mainland, had gotten a plane ticket back.

Once he paid the bill and insisted that she take her uneaten food to go, he got in the truck and offered to drive her back after he dumped off the kayaks.

"No, I can walk back," she said.

"It's over four miles in the dark. I just don't think it's safe."

"Oh, I've walked farther than that in the dark. I'm not afraid."

"Let me drive you, please."

Duke couldn't let this woman go. There was something about her that was compelling to him. She seemed soft and vulnerable, yet she was close to his age. She seemed untouched by life, so innocent.

She climbed in his van and he drove her back past homes that sat on the Smuggler's Cove beach built in the genre of *Life Styles of the Rich and Famous*, aping television mansions with pink stucco walls. There sat string after string of big homes on lots so small that even the gentrified mortgagee, while sitting on his commode, had only to pull up his window shade to peer at his neighbor who was engaged in the same task. Slowly the land grew sparse, filled only with thorn trees and crows as they veered over the lava roads. The sun was going down against flamboyant orange clouds in a periwinkle sky as they pulled into the same spot where he had found her.

She ran to her dugout and made a quick inventory. Everything was still there, even her rooster. She turned to smile at him. Then she got back into the car.

"You've been very kind to me. Don't you have a girlfriend who is waiting for you?"

Duke took her in his arms and before he could answer, she dipped her head and unfastened his trousers. This caused him to slump a little in his seat. Her head made a simple gesture like a bird going after seed or water. His protuberance gave way to a big orgasm within seconds.

He laughed heartily afterwards. "Hey, I heard there are ninety grams of protein in that."

Her eyes were wide, looking straight at him. She gulped, as if she was swallowing a smoothie filled with Spirulina, and then she giggled. Her femininity was intense.

He felt that she seemed like a disoriented little girl. She had lost her way and all he wanted to do was make things right for her. His heart ached so for her lonely life. He held her. She kissed him with appreciation. He let himself down on the ground still warmed by the daytime sun and caressed her. He let her lead him to her nest, and he found himself making love to her. He had never felt so much tenderness in a woman he barely knew. She was healing his wounded soul. It made no sense to him several hours later when he took leave of her, hopped into his truck and drove home. Who could have imagined that his day would end with this interlude?

Delila was waiting for him with a cold dinner. She seemed to accept his vague excuse about tourist delays, high surf and traffic. That night he slept peacefully in the hands of a world that lay spread out around him like a bewildering and stupendous dream. Next to him Delila sat awake with her eyes wide open, counting the dots on the white asbestos ceiling squares.

15

"I think I have carpal tunnel. I can't move my fingers and wrist," Ralph reported to the group the morning after the first evening session, when Yogianni and Sky gave their Amrita demonstration. It was after breakfast during the circle sharing.

"My jaw also feels a little sore," he continued, rubbing the palm of his hand back and forth under his chin.

He turned toward Sky and said, "A full evening of diddle-dology really did me in. My wife almost had to rush me to the emergency room last night."

Paula gave Ralph a disgusted look. His humor was embarrassing. She wanted all of them to think that she was the stellar student, along with Ralph. Why did he have to act like such a jerk at crucial times?

Sky smiled patronizingly as he adjusted his legs in his Back-To-The-Earth pants so that he could sit in a more comfortable lotus position at the front of the room. That's what happens when you throw pearls to swine, he thought. He felt unappreciated and hurt, though he threw a winning smile to Ralph and Paula across the room. He had helped so many people over the years discover their sexual potential that he hated being joked about.

Money comes easily and effortlessly to me. At least I'm getting paid big bucks for being The Tantric God, and I *live in paradise,* affirmed Sky silently. After all, he had the lifestyle he wanted: money and nubile women lusting after him. Yogianni had been very juicy at first, but like all women, she had just become a moneymaker for him. He was surprised that she stuck around. It was to her credit that she knew her role, and she was a good advertisement for his business. He knew that he could be very demanding and uncompromising, but she kept loving him despite his behavior, which included disappearing for days at a time, and then arriving with young, soft-skinned waifs. He looked across at Ralph again and had to remind himself that Ralph was of no consequence.

Delila had stationed herself deliberately next to Ralph, and she found that she liked his irreverence, although she rolled her eyes in a look of faked hopelessness of the male species. Nevertheless, she noticed how radiant Paula and Ralph looked this morning, and she felt a bit envious.

The first evening session had been a disaster for her and Duke. He refused to come out from under the covers when their sexual assistant, Yogianni, slipped into their room after midnight. It wasn't that Duke was impotent. He just had old-fashioned values. For Delila, he represented the Wild West she had always dreamed about.

Yogianni had to forcibly rip the duvet off the bed to get Duke to participate. Delila was livid with embarrassment. After all, Delila *was* a transformational dance therapist and had her reputation to keep on this small island. What would happen if it got out that Duke had locked himself in the bathroom after Yogianni's brief visit? Delila found out the next morning that he had slept in the tub with only some towels for a headrest.

He told her, "I just couldn't get it up last night, honey. I'm not used to more than one woman at a time." It was an embarrassment of riches, he had said sheepishly. "It just doesn't salute on command!"

Truth be told, she thought, he had been mediocre for awhile. Maybe it was the money pressure of living on an island where granola cost twelve dollars a box. Maybe if they were married things would change. If they didn't change soon, she wouldn't be able to hold her head up at Dance Spirit on Friday nights. Delila had learned quickly that living on an island wasn't at all like living on the mainland. It was downright primitive in some ways, unlike Steamboat, where Duke was the owner of the Jelly Roll Café.

Delila was thinking of the time she told Miracle that she was sick and then showed up at a party. Friends gossiped. There were no secrets, not even about Duke's sex life. She could imagine the gossip: Stud Muffin on the outside, Putz Muffin on the inside. She couldn't bear it. She immediately channeled Ariel, her special spiritual guide, to change her bad thoughts into good ones.

Across the room, Paula was reflecting on how different last night with Ralph had been. Usually she woke at three o'clock in the morning, worrying about her show or her book. He was always on edge about whether he'd be fired for being too old or too gray or too controversial in his clients' buttoned-down-corporate world. She hadn't felt such gentleness towards him in several years. She loved the softness of their cuddling afterwards. Ralph, too, seemed renewed and in good spirits.

Last night, toward the end, she had picked up a weird vibe from Yogianni of some attraction toward Ralph, but maybe that was her paranoia, or she was just tired from so much happening in one twenty-four hour period. After all, they had never done anything quite like this before. They didn't have much experience with dope or any drugs. While others marched, revolted, smoked, dropped acid and generally transformed and reinvented themselves, Ralph and Paula were working away in the corporate world. Ralph had avoided the draft by going back to school, and Paula had been focused on advancing in her career.

Despite her strong woman's liberation orientation, suddenly she thought that she couldn't have been in her right mind letting Yogianni into their bedroom last night. Yogianni seemed almost too serious about her work. Paula decided that she needed to keep her eye out for her.

Another thing, these people seemed to do pot the way she ate potato chips. Maybe they even did other drugs. They just didn't run in those circles, although in the right circumstances, she was game.

Sky announced that today the group was headed for Tantric on the beach. The guys were going to go separately from the gals and meet up at the designated spot. The gals were going to pick up lunch and do some errands on the way. Yogianni took her own truck and was going to meet them there. She had stuff to prepare for the workshop and the upcoming wedding of Miracle and Reefdancer. She hoped that she could find a way to be alone with Ralph on the beach.

Duke loaded the kayaks on top of his SUV and convinced everyone to meet him down at the boat launch near Brewer's Bay. This was where he had spotted spinner dolphins in the open ocean on his recent trip as a tour guide.

Ralph, Duke, Antonio and Reefdancer jumped into Duke's SUV. Ralph took one last, longing look at Delila in her bikini with the green and gold sarong wrapped around her thin waist. He was fantasizing about what it would be like to spend quality time with her.

Paula, Miracle and Delila promised to be along shortly. They were going to meet the guys down at the beach, but first Miracle had to check her phone messages at her colonic studio. She had to do callbacks to eager tourists at a nearby hotel. Delila went to pick up lunch supplies for the group at the strip mall.

Delila drove into the deli parking lot, deep in thought. She was thinking about how paradise, with its balmy air, swaying palm trees, and long white stretches of beach, became just another shantytown when the sun went in and the dark clouds stretched across the island. She hated the humidity when the wind stopped blowing. When all was said and done, it was a rock a thousand miles away from anywhere. And there was no good shopping!

She didn't seem to be having much fun in her life these days, and she came here to be "in the fun zone." She definitely planned to confide in her best friend, Miracle, about this. Miracle was an advocate of the vacation lifestyle. She would understand.

Delila wanted to keep up with her friends. She had brought up marriage to Duke once again last night. He had said dreamily, "You know, honey, I've been married four times before. You could kind of say I'm a veteran. Please don't ask me again. Let me just wake up one morning and turn to you and say, 'Honey, today's the day to get us married.' That's how I want to do it this time."

She was thinking about how romantic that would be when she was jarred back to reality. Delila almost collided with a blue Ford Sentra as she shot in front of his car and grabbed the only empty parking space.

After gathering lunch supplies, she swung around to pick up Miracle and Paula, but before she opened the passenger door for them, she quickly took off the dust cover of the book she had been reading, *Couples For Keeps* by Dr. Snookie McGants, the psychologist on the Oprah Winfrey show. The book flew into the back seat, away from prying eyes, and the dust cover slid under the driver's seat. No one noticed. Paula was in her own world, gazing out the window.

She was worrying about the status of her book and if it had found a publishing home. She had gotten so tied up in this sex workshop that it slipped her mind to even call her agent. She reminded herself of the difference in time zones and wondered if her cell phone would even work. If the book didn't get published, it would make her work so much harder because it wouldn't give her the visibility that only a book could. She hated when she got anxious, and she thought of those little blue pills she had brought. But they were stashed away in her carry-on, back at the workshop along with her cell phone. The pills and the call would have to wait until later.

"I asked him about marriage last night, and he gave me the most romantic reassurance I've ever heard." Delila's words came out in a raspy high whine, not very convincing to Miracle, as she had barely gotten into the car, closed the door and nodded to Paula. They were headed to meet the group waiting for them on the beach.

Miracle, who was five years younger than Delila and many pounds heavier, took the bull by the horns. Sometimes she felt like Delila's big sister. Hadn't she taken Goddess Empowerment Training from the experts? She knew when she had putty in her hands. Delila was ready to be molded.

"Well, the answer to that question of marriage is either yes or no," Miracle said. "What do you want the answer to be?"

"I want someone to take care of me and I want to be famous, well, like Sky and Yogianni."

"They're not exactly what you'd call Fame-ous."

"Oh, you know what I mean, but everyone knows them." *Miracle is acting like a real know-it-all*, thought Delila.

Miracle thought of Delila's answering machine message and web page: "This is Delila Courtney Loveland, you have reached Transformation in Paradise: the home of satisfying sexual healing, Ethereal Dance, Breakthrough Empowerment Seminars and Wellbeing Housecleaning Service."

It did seem like Delila wanted everything and just didn't know how to focus!

At least Miracle had a boyfriend who owned a real ranch with horses, and he knew everyone on the island. Well, he knew all the women because he had slept with each one at one time or another since 1960. But everyone agreed that she had caught a Big Fish. She only wished that she didn't have to work. She thought that when they married, she could quit her job. She had gotten him to agree on their wedding taking place during the workshop. That was a coup! That way only the "right" people would be there. Sky and Yogianni thought that was a great way to celebrate a Tantric sex couple, which they were, and all the participants were invited. For Reefdancer, the annulment of his first marriage took longer than the marriage itself, which had lasted only a week and a day.

"We had such a luscious time last night," Miracle confided to Delila. "He said he wouldn't make me sign a prenuptial agreement!"

Delila bristled inside. "Fun Zone!"

"Reefdancer not only found my G spot, but we also spent some time in the other places. You should have seen the Amrita *flow!*" Miracle elongated the word to stress her success.

"Well, Duke and I are *very sexual* ourselves, that isn't a problem. And Yogianni came by to assist."

Miracle knew that tone.

Delila stared ahead, seething. Just because Miracle was a colonic therapist, she acted like she knew every sexual secret known to mankind. You'd think she was a medical doctor at times, by the way she talked about things. Like how Miracle and Reefdancer boasted to everyone about their love days of "spiritual and sexual healing." At that moment she decided not to confide in Miracle any more.

"Yogianni? That's a joke," screamed Miracle. "She's totally, I mean *totally* non-orgasmic. That's why she hangs out with Sky."

Paula gasped from the back seat. The other two women looked at her.

"She came to our room last night and helped Ralph and me. Are you sure? She sure had me fooled!"

"What do you mean?" Miracle asked curiously.

"Well, look at her demonstration in the group and all that goopy stuff. She must have been orgasming."

"Au contraire, little grasshopper," Miracle giggled. She twisted her body to face Paula in the back seat. "You can be filled with Amrita, but that doesn't mean you are orgasming."

"You can be enjoying yourself, though," added Delila, laughing.

"Or not," Miracle told her. "Sometimes touching the G spot can feel very painful if you are uptight or not relaxed enough or have been wounded sexually or abused as a girl. It is pleasuring but not orgasming. How about you? Do you have love days with Ralph?"

"Well, no," Paula volunteered honestly. She felt a little ashamed, even though it crossed her mind that she didn't know exactly what love days entailed.

She asked, "What do you both do on a love day? I mean, all day long you make love? How about eating? Or errands?"

Miracle answered, "Well, we pleasure one another all day. I mean we wake up and give each other baths and long luxurious massages. Sometimes I give him a colonic and he gives me one. He loves that, because that's how we first met. I prepare a special meal and we feed each other. We dress up in costumes. I've collected lots of outfits over the years, so we become other people and turn each other on. Several times we've even played with different kinds of vegetables."

"Like what?"

"Zucchinis or small eggplants are the best organic vibrators."

Miracle and Delila burst into laughter. Paula thought for a moment that it was their own private joke.

"No, I mean the costumes, like what?"

"Captain Kid and Pocahontas, or even Little Red Riding Hood and the Big Bad Wolf. We got a lot of mileage out of that one. Then we make love slowly and consciously. We might take a walk and find a place to do it in the meadow. We might spread out a blanket and bring some vitamin e or wine."

"Vitamin e?"

"That's what we call the love drug Ecstasy. Have you ever taken it?"

"No."

"It opens your heart and you love everything and everyone."

"They should put it in the drinking water of the island," added Delila. "Do you have days like that?"

During Miracle and Reefdancer's sexual marathons, their bed swung heavily from the ceiling smack in the middle of the living room, with an enormous crystal lying on the purple velvet duvet that sucked up all the bad energy in the room.

In the past several months, Delila had come home and wanted love days with Duke. He joked around about it and then fell silent, engrossed in pro football on television. Later he napped, dead to the world, on the living room sofa.

"Sure," answered Delila, trying to keep up sexually.

"I don't have anything like it in my life," Paula said wistfully, feeling a little competitive. "You know, I have to produce a television show and Ralph is pretty busy with his work as a creative director for an advertising agency, so we don't seem to be in the bed at the same time often." Paula was never at a loss for one-upmanship. If not in the sexual arena, she could find it in her work. But in this conversation she felt at a loss to share similar experiences.

"You do television? Wow? What show?"

"It's just one show on discovering people who used to be famous and interviewing them. You'd be surprised how curious people are about other people's lives and what they have done with them."

"Oh, I could introduce you to some people here on the island who really were famous in the 'sixties," volunteered Delila.

"Yeah, like who? " asked Miracle.

"You remember Dr. Jacobs, who had that television show about sex? He was really popular, then he got very controversial and finally he got kicked off the island."

"Dr. Jacobs?" Paula was stunned.

"Yeah. I wonder what he is doing now? Yogianni and he were close for quite awhile. In fact, that's how she hooked up with Sky. He was a friend of Dr. Jacobs' from the East Coast. Sky had a falling-out with him. They became very competitive with each other."

"Is he a baldish guy with very penetrating eyes, and he licks his lips a lot?"

"Yeah, that sounds like him," Delila said.

"He's my gynecologist in Marin!"

They all were silenced by the revelation.

Paula broke the silence. "What was the controversy?"

"So that's where he landed, eh?" Miracle said. "Well, let's just say that he gave his patients a lot for their money."

Delila snickered.

"No, seriously, some said that he gave them an oral sexual experience that they would never forget right in his office."

Paula gulped. "Did it ever happen to you?"

"Not me, but some of my pretty close friends. He actually was a pretty good gynecologist," Delila said. "Good bedside manner." She giggled.

"He was my doctor when he lived here," said Miracle. "It really was sad. He was quite the celebrity."

"You know Miracle and Reefdancer will be getting married before you leave," said Delila.

"I'd love you both to come to our wedding. It's going to be tropical style," Miracle said.

"Sure, I'm sure Ralph would love to."

"I am so happy that you and Ralph will be at my wedding. We don't usually have many celebrities of our own here." Miracle turned to the back seat, addressing Paula and trying to avoid further tension with Delila.

"Well, I'm not exactly a celebrity, but I do know, shall we say, people who used to be celebrities."

Miracle knew Delila well enough to know that she would try to take over Paula with name-dropping, so Paula might get interested in her and want to meet some of those people. Delila would make Paula think that only she had access to important people on the island, of course. Delila might even try to get on Paula's show. Miracle needed to be part of that action.

Paula was pleased that she might make a find or two on the island before she left, and she was oblivious to the tensions going on between Delila and Miracle, since they were strangers to her.

Delila looked spitefully at Miracle. At least *she* wasn't overweight. She still had her thick, long, blonde hair and well-shaped breasts. She got a lot of compliments on those babies. Sometimes she would even find men talking to her cleavage. That always struck her kind of funny.

As they got off the highway and onto the city streets of Tortola, they passed a woman in her fifties with sun-bleached hair, walking along the street pushing a Happy Food Market shopping cart. Piled high in disarray were all her worldly goods. She appeared to have been a beauty at one time. Today she was wearing a satin oyster colored wedding dress with a tattered train. A live, crowing, red rooster preened himself atop her cart.

"Hey there's Fawn! Stop the car!" shouted Miracle. "Roll down the window."

Delila slowed down to wave. Fawn waved back and kept walking along, her dirty train following behind on the dusty shoulder of the road, her bare swollen feet protruding from under the long hem.

Delila let out a sigh. She wanted to get to the beach and be with the guys. This day was not turning out like she had planned. Miracle had taken entirely too long getting ready, and now she had to stop.

"Hey, Fawn," shouted Miracle. "What's happening?"

Fawn smiled wide, showing a full set of teeth with the middle front one missing. "I'm just going to meet a friend," she shouted.

"We're on our way to meet our guys on the beach." Miracle leaned over Delila to get a better look. She wanted Fawn to know about her wedding.

"Do you know Delila, Duke's partner?"

Fawn took a step back, and her smile faded. She suddenly realized that the man whom she met on the beach the other day was with this woman.

"You mean Duke, the guide."

"Yeah."

"I met him yesterday."

Delila flashed a smile she didn't mean. "Sorry, honey, but we gotta go, we got some people waiting for us," she said impatiently and sped off.

"I wanted to tell her about our wedding," said Miracle.

"You can call her," answered Delila.

"Right, she has a cell phone in her shopping cart?"

"Were you going to invite her, anyway?"

The strangely attired woman had aroused Paula's curiosity. "What's her story?"

"Don't you know?"

"C'mon, how the hell would she know?"

"Oh, all right. She's Sky's wife. He left her with nothing and moved in with Yogianni about ten years ago. So Fawn went to Hollywood to become a star, but I don't think she was all that successful. It did something to her head. I haven't seen her in awhile. But she sleeps on the beach. I know that because I've seen her just waking up during my early morning jogs there."

"Isn't that dangerous?" Paula leaned forward from the back seat.

"She told me that she locks herself in the women's room on the beach at night to sleep. But it isn't safe. Drugs and stuff."

Delila shuddered. "The woman has become a bag lady. Why doesn't Sky do something?"

There was a moment of silence. It occurred to both of the Tortola women that this could be a glimpse into their future if they didn't play their cards right. Unlike Paula, they didn't have an education or experience as a seasoned career woman.

This encounter affected Paula strangely. Here in paradise it had appeared that all one's needs were taken care of; but Paula was changing her mind.

"What can he do? She seems happy enough," Miracle said.

As Delila pulled away from the curb, she felt very disturbed, but she tried to hide it from her girlfriend and Paula. She knew that she must find time to speak to Duke about this. Why hadn't he told her about meeting Fawn? From experience, when men didn't tell you about meeting another woman, it wasn't innocent. What did Duke have to hide? She realized that Duke had some explaining to do. The day was definitely deteriorating.

16

Exactly at the same time, but several miles back up the road, in Duke's red jeep, the guys were careening down the highway past Road Town Market to meet the girls on the designated beach. Ralph saw wind surfers skimming the waves like monarch butterflies. The watery expanse of ocean lay as flat and calm as a frozen pond, while the sun was already ablaze in the early morning sky.

Ralph was thinking about how this remote tropical island lay so far away from his home in California. At that moment he felt precarious, like a speck on the planet Earth. He was thinking that maybe he could forget about his feelings of captivity and try to enjoy himself.

When they arrived at the beach and were reunited with their partners and Yogianni, Paula saw a sight that she had never seen before off in the distance. Huge gray forms of ocean life were surging out of the water with the grace of ballerinas, six or seven at a time, the sunlight reflected off their backs as they surfaced and then plunged deep below. Again and again they would reemerge and plunge, like horses on a carousel.

Sky shouted and pointed toward the reef, "The dolphins are back, the dolphins are back!"

Quickly, the group poured into kayaks and tied their mesh snorkel and fin bags to side straps to hold them securely. Sky lingered behind, screwing up his courage, because no one knew that he didn't know how to swim.

The smell of the salt air and the sound of the sea birds made Paula tingle. She saw Duke's muscles ripple with the backbreaking task of pushing each kayak out into the ocean against the resistance of the incoming waves.

She loved the sight of his strength, but it was only an intellectual love. She couldn't imagine herself with him. Her admiration came out of the sense of one looking at Michelangelo's *David*, or Rodin's *The Thinker*. She would never risk an advance towards him for fear of rejection. She knew that she had already gone too far in the last few days, and she would be playing with fire if she moved towards Duke.

With Paula in front and Ralph steering in the back, they paddled across the incoming surf, following their chain of five kayaks out into open ocean.

Last night's sexual escapades were a distant memory, as the coastline of coral reefs disappeared. Paula surprised herself by thinking that Dr. Jacobs, despite his seedy background, was probably right. A trip like this was changing her negative attitude toward Ralph.

All they could hear now was the lapping of water against the sides of their hulls, the rush of the wind, the sound of seagulls overhead, and the roar of a light plane flying a banner advertising a tee-shirt outlet in town.

A calm enveloped the group as they followed Duke in the head canoe.

"Look Paula, those fish, the coral reefs," Ralph shouted to

her, but his words were swallowed up in the rush of the wind and surf around them.

"Swim, swim," yelled Sky as Duke and Yogianni hastily put on their gear and jumped recklessly overboard to keep up with the dolphins. Everyone except Sky followed.

Swimming in the ocean freestyle, even with fins, took more strength than Paula had because of all the swells. Chasing the ever-widening circle of bottlenose dolphins made her tired within several minutes. Duke was the first to give up the chase and pull himself into his kayak.

She leisurely breast-stroked back to the side of Duke's kayak and hung on the side enjoying the warm sun, the coolness of the early morning water and the strength of Duke's tanned body.

Duke was enjoying his role as the spotter. Like a traffic director, he had an aerial view and shouted out where the dolphins were surfacing next.

"They are at two o'clock," he yelled, and suddenly everyone changed direction and began swimming fiercely towards the creatures to get a closer look. It was hard to tell one person from another behind their masks and snorkel equipment.

Ralph began to hang back and slow down. He initially had been focusing his eyes on the dolphins, but as his swimming got slower and more relaxed, he began seeing huge green sea turtles wedged against large outcroppings of coral. Some had barnacles covering their shells and thick fins. When he looked down into the coral, he saw an octopus in slow motion moving between the rocks. It occurred to him that this was the first time in many weeks that he was completely enjoying the moment.

Just as quickly as the dolphins came, they disappeared.

"Let's go to the aquarium," Duke announced. Once the entourage was back in their kayaks, with snorkel and fins stored, they began paddling with the current to the other side of the bay. As they got closer, Paula observed how small and unsafe she felt, especially as she saw the waves crashing against the jagged cliffs and outcropping of rocks near the shore. If she hadn't been in the confident hands of Duke in the lead, she felt she surely would not survive.

She thought of how rowing this kayak with Ralph was a real metaphor for their lives together. Each had to keep up efforts to help the other or they would sink.

Duke guided them across a coral reef, and the waters got shallower and shallower. Ralph leaned over the side of the boat to point out coral, the color of amber, puce and burnt sienna. Green sea turtles covered with algae, the size of compact cars, lounged under mushroom-shaped coral formations.

"This is just like skiing," observed Ralph. "It's so smooth, like glass at points. You could almost walk over it."

The aquarium served as a snorkeling place for the locals, safe from tourists: difficult to get to by foot since it was a three-mile walk on uneven rocky ground or a long paddle from the neighboring shore.

This was where Reefdancer and Miracle, Antonio and his women went to spend a day after taking Ecstasy. Locals lovingly called it vitamin e. This was their drug of choice and a staple amongst the locals who had arrived in the late 'sixties and stayed to raise families and grow old.

Ralph watched in awe the variety of fish that swam by: blue Parrotfish, Christmas Wrasses, and Moorish Idols. "These are the kind of fish you only see at the aquarium in Fong Tins Chinese Restaurant," Ralph whispered to Paula. She was too busy rowing and keeping up with Duke to hear Ralph's observation.

Sky, Yogianni and Antonio had found a baby turtle with a hook and line in its fin, left by some fishermen. Surprisingly, the creature stopped flailing long enough to let the men take the hook out. It dove underwater almost immediately.

"That hook could have caused that little guy to drown if he got caught under a rock," Sky said to the waiting group sunning themselves on shore.

He dug into his airtight bag and pulled out some Balance bars for everyone. It was only nine o'clock in the morning. They had been gone two hours.

Yogianni gathered the group around her. "Today we are in the most spacious and lovely place on earth, and to enhance this beauty we'll all take vitamin e. That's Ecstasy, a most powerful chemical aphrodisiac. I suggest that you drink a full glass of water and find a place to lie down for awhile."

Paula went off to lie on the sand. The vitamin e began working and she could feel all her negative feelings dissipate as Ralph lay next to her. He became a being in pure white light. Her heart felt like it would burst with love, while her skin tingled and all she could feel was the need to be touched. She felt so aroused. She wrapped her muddy legs around Ralph. They both were enveloped in a soft pillow of transparent, flimsy unreality. All she heard was the sound of the lapping water and the smell of salt air. A thought flitted across Paula's mind, a tune from *South Pacific*.

Ralph forgot about the surroundings and the other couples whispering, laughing and making love in the clay nearby. He felt contented, like a baby, in the sheer physical enjoyment of Paula's body, a voluptuous female body that was pleasuring him. It was plump. He was getting into her plumpness. It was not a vital part of her body, this cushiony feeling, but why, he wondered, at this moment was he willing to sell his soul for her plumpness? He suddenly felt the urge and wanted Paula to go down on him and lick his cock. He pushed her head toward his member, but she looked up bewildered.

"I just can't do that."

"What?" He had never in all their years of marriage asked her to do this. Now he wondered why. It would be so pleasurable for him. They had done it earlier in their court-ship. Why would she deny him?

"Do I have to swallow?"

"I don't care," he answered exasperatedly.

"I just can't." She gasped for air.

"Why?"

"Well, I'm not sure you want to know. I never told you this, but when I was fifteen, the minister at our church invited the West Point Jewish Choir to our temple for a Friday night service. Twenty-five gorgeous older boys arrived. They all were in uniforms and had crew cuts. I couldn't tell one from another."

"Why the hell are you telling me this story now?" Ralph pondered as he saw the sun shifting in the sky.

"Shut up and listen! I found one guy that I thought was really attractive, but I kept losing sight of him, because they all looked so much alike. Finally, that night we got to dance together, and he took me home."

Ralph was thinking that maybe he'd never remember the exact location of the G spot. His member was slowly shrinking the more she expounded.

"When we got near my house, he slowed and then stopped the car. We started making out and it was really juicy. Slowly he began pushing my head down toward his crotch while he unzipped his pants, just like now."

Ralph was thinking that maybe he hadn't learned anything really last night, that he blew the money on Yogianni and this whole thing, and that he couldn't even get a decent blow job.

"He pulled out his cock and asked me to put it in my mouth. Now remember, I was a virgin, and I didn't know that anything actually came out of it but pee. So when he let out a huge moan moments later, and then came, I just gagged and spewed it all over him."

Ralph cracked up laughing. All these years and he had never heard this before. "You'd think I'd know all of your stories by now."

"The guy was so ashamed. He said that I must think he was an animal and didn't know how to behave. I must have done something right, because weeks later, he asked me up to West Point for a weekend, and my mother let me go and I went. I guess I was curious about the next chapter because when I got there, I found a whole different world than my little town."

"Like what?" Now Ralph was getting interested. His cock had lost interest entirely.

"There were these guys in uniforms running around this gothic-looking campus, and they all carried attaché cases, as if they carried the code to the nuclear bomb in them. The girls had curfews and were brought back to several guest homes run by old spinsters outside the campus, and there was a pecking order. The most popular girls from various colleges in the area were the ones who sported big engagement rings and were planning their weddings, then came ones like us, first or second timers. We all had to board a bus and were driven to the campus morning, noon and night. Everything was so structured.

"What I didn't realize until too late was that these guys had one thing on their mind and one thing only. In each of their attaché cases were condoms and a blanket. We spent the whole weekend looking for vacant broom closets, empty classrooms, barns, behind closed doors and coat closets in which to fuck and suck. Sometimes we'd open the door of a remote location, and we'd find one of the girls with one of those big engagement rings and her cadet locked in a passionate embrace. So that was the weekend I learned how to give head. I really lost my taste for it after that. I guess I could try it again."

Ralph paused and considered. "No, that's okay."

It may have been the drugs, but it seemed to Ralph that so much of the female anatomy was always in motion, giggling, hiding or elusive. The gold member could most often be counted on. It was either on or off. The G spot seemed to keep moving around. One thing was for sure, he would always enjoy the female body. It was soft as a pillow, slowly aroused, teased and prodded. In contrast, his muscles were dense and firm. His fingers were like the sides of mutton, so technically he wasn't a pro, but hey, his instrument still worked. Didn't Paula always say that enlightenment was just being in Buddha Mind, accepting what was? And on this sunny day that was all that mattered.

Paula began to feel silly nude. A wind came up, it was getting chilly, and everyone was drifting back to the boats. So she decided to get dressed.

Sky started rounding up the last of the bedraggled, sex-besotted group and they got into their kayaks and went out the rivulets over the coral, single file, the way they had come in.

Back in the boats now, it was harder to paddle. Paula and Ralph were struggling.

"We are paddling against the current," Duke yelled as he pulled past them. Big swells yanked the kayak up and down. Then his boat slipped back again.

"I'm pooped," yelled Paula to Ralph. Her arms ached, but the beauty around her, and the vitamin e, helped her forget her pain.

She could see whitecaps and feel the choppy water beneath her kayak. The ocean had changed its mood while they were on the shore, and Paula was feeling some strangeness in her stomach. Seasickness was taking shape.

She looked ahead at the kayaks in front of her. The others, too, were paddling hard. The sky darkened as the clouds passed over the sun.

The Tortola Cloud that Sky had told them about hung over the mountain, causing an overcast sky by mid-morning.

Without warning, Sky stood up in his boat as if to change paddles and then fell overboard into the churning sea. Ralph saw Sky drift away flailing against the current. Rapidly, it took him back downwind.

Without a moment's hesitation, Ralph dove into the water as Paula screeched with horror. He swam toward Sky, who was flailing furiously and taking in water. The other men sat and watched in a vitamin e haze. Within seconds, Ralph had the unconscious Sky on his back and was hauling him toward Duke's kayak. Duke tried to maintain the stability of the boat while he threw out an inflated cushion and Ralph grasped onto it with Sky and hoisted him into the boat. Ralph followed.

Once on shore, everyone gathered around Sky as Ralph administered mouth-to-mouth resuscitation. Seawater spewed out of Sky's mouth. Paula had never seen Ralph respond so fast. She knew he was a good athlete, but he never rippled his muscles or flaunted it in front of people. And he had never been the kind of guy who offered to lug someone's couch upstairs. The lifesaving and mouth-to-mouth resuscitation he had learned as the safety captain at work now came in handy. She stood back with amazement and pride at his quick thinking.

Everyone patted him on the back. Then Duke pushed Ralph out of the way. "We've got to get him to the emergency room quickly."

Antonio intervened, "But that's about forty-five minutes away, or even an hour at this hour with the traffic on the main road."

Yogianni stood on the shore paralyzed and weeping quietly.

The mood of celebration that accompanied the group these last twenty-four hours was gone. A somber tone took its place, as they wondered if Sky was going to make it. They still hadn't realized that he didn't know how to swim.

17

"It seems like our vacation has taken a strange turn," Ralph whispered to Paula as Antonio and Reefdancer carried Sky to Duke's red jeep. Ralph was upset that he had gone along with this adventure. It had really gone too far.

Paradise had not been designed to accommodate a tragedy; that's why it was called paradise. Even at dusk, as if on purpose, the landscape held no looming shadows and no gaunt silhouettes. It was invincibly cheerful, a toyland of exotic flora and pastel stucco houses lived in by transplants whose bright, uncurtained windows winked blandly through a dappling of magenta, crimson and periwinkle blossoms.

If a man running down the road was in desperate grief he would be indecently out of place.

Paula was so proud that Ralph had stepped up to take charge. Yogianni stood at his side waiting for the next set of instructions. She was still crying.

Sky had looked ashen and unconscious. "We better get him over to Allen," Reefdancer said. "Allen is doing a session down at Frank Fagioli's, it's the closest place."

"Is he the local doctor?" asked Paula.

"No actually, he's a psychic healer who's come up from Rio," Yogianni said. "Take him there."

"That and a dollar will get you a cup of coffee," Duke said as he got into his vehicle and started it up. "You win."

Paula had read about psychic healers before, but had never actually been in the presence of one.

"Shouldn't you take him to the emergency room?" Ralph asked. It seemed like a strange place to take a guy who was semi-conscious, but this was the Caribbean. They must know something I don't, he thought. His patience was wearing thin with this group. Who's the adult here? he wondered. I guess it's me.

Ralph looked at Paula. She looked back at him with a little smile and shrugged her shoulders. Oh, she's having a ball, he thought. An I-got-to-get-out-of-here feeling surged again in Ralph. His leadership instincts were dwindling.

They drove down the rutted dirt road that ran along the shore. Here, the houses got larger, with security fences and metal electronic gates facing the street. The backs of the homes lined a private ocean beach.

Ralph's eyes bulged. Each house was more beautiful than the next and surrounded by lush jacaranda trees, gigantic bird of paradise and brilliant flowering bougainvillea. The beach-clad tribe pulled into a driveway and Reefdancer got out and pressed the buttons on the electronic code box, as if he lived there. The gate opened slowly.

They drove to the front of the mansion.

Miracle, sensing Paula was bewildered, filled her in, while Ralph and the others carried Sky into the house. Yogianni was at his side and attending to him fastidiously.

"Dr. Botox is really Allen. I mean, he channels Dr. Botox, a famous German doctor who died a century ago. Well, Allen was discovered by Frank Fagioli, the man that owns this estate.

Famous healers pass through these parts all the time. Frank Fagioli usually bankrolls the best ones. I mean there was Boomba-gee, and Tapa Tool Das. Each has an important message to teach about reaching enlightenment. But Dr. Botox, I mean Allen, is really the best."

Paula looked past Miracle to several dark-skinned servants dressed in white uniforms and aprons, then past them to the surf crashing against the rocks, which was Frank Fagioli's back yard.

"Who *is* this guy?" asked Ralph, returning from inside. The place was opulent, with oversized chandeliers, vast rooms with vaulted ceilings and upholstered mahogany furniture.

"He's this really wealthy Italian guy who has bought up most of Tortola and even took over the local newspaper, when it almost went under," Delila said. "You'll get to meet him if he's home. You may have seen him on the beach when you arrived. He's a short, fat, bald guy with hair growing out of his nose. I see him walking on Josiah's Bay beach every morning. He's usually arm in arm with a young girl he brings over from Eastern Europe. I didn't know he was so loaded or I would have claimed him for myself."

Duke joined the conversation. "You ought to see him early in the morning on the beach!"

Everyone looked at him quizzically and Duke explained. "The guy is so cheap, he walks the public beaches with a metal detector early before the sun comes up, combing for loose change from tourists."

Ralph laughed. "You must be joking?"

"No, it's true. Ask anyone. Yet, with all his money, he can't get a woman, so he sponsors beauty contests in Eastern Europe, the prize winner gets to come to Tortola, and guess what the prize is?" Duke paused. "Frank Fagioli! The contest winner gets to live with Frank Fagioli! Of course, he paints a totally different picture of the scene to the women who win. But that's until he gets tired of them."

"About three months is all it takes," Delila said, nodding. "Of course he'd never tire of me," she added, giggling.

"Sexual slaves?" Paula was incredulous.

"Not exactly. He sends them back when they want. They aren't hostages."

"Whatta guy," said Ralph admiringly. *These guys have a lot of time on their hands*, he thought.

"Not really," said Miracle. "What woman wouldn't want to come to America? The reason Allen is here is that Frank Fagioli smuggled him out of Brazil to heal one of his Eastern European prizewinners when she had a cancer scare. Allen was viewed as an enemy of the new regime. She met Allen when he came to her country, Chechnya or one of those little war-torn countries. He's in session now. You'll both get to see his healing powers. He is miraculous!"

At that moment a smiling man of about thirty-two stepped out of the open French doors and waved them inside. It was Allen. He had dyed and gelled platinum hair that stood up in spikes. He wore a tropical-style shirt open to his waist and three gold chains around his neck. His black chest hairs, like Brillo, pushed out from beneath. He could have stepped right out of *The Young and the Restless* or *Dallas*.

His eyes penetrated right through Paula and it suddenly occurred to her that he'd be pretty conspicuous to smuggle out, unless someone drugged him and threw him into a gunnysack and dumped him into the belly of the plane. She wondered if the story was true, or if it just added to his mystery.

In the darkened living room, forty or so men and women in loose fitting clothes sat in lotus position. They had their eyes closed and were emitting a loud humming sound in unison. Sky had been placed supine and spread-eagled in the center of the room, attended to by several women. His eyes were closed. Allen assumed a cross-legged position at his side.

Paula noticed a medicinal smell as she quietly joined the circle with the others. She wondered anxiously if Sky was going to die or survive this strange ordeal. The others seemed very calm, except Ralph, who fidgeted. Paula was anxious about this use of non-traditional medicine to heal someone who might have a concussion or dehydration. How could these people so innocently believe this voodoo?

"The incense in this room is killing me," Ralph whispered loudly and began sniffling.

Allen motioned for some women who were standing in a corner of the room to come to his aid. Each carried a bowl filled with liquid and white towels.

They knelt at his side. Meanwhile, another woman walked around the inside of the group, encouraging the participants to keep up the humming by repeating a mantra she was singing. She seemed like the starter act on a dinner show at Vegas because she was dressed in flowing orange and blue silk scarves with lots of necklaces and huge, silver drop earrings. She bent down to touch some women and to encourage the men to sing louder. Ralph couldn't make out the exact words. They didn't sound like English but some strange combination of words. He could neither catch nor repeat them on command. He tried to sit silently and forget about the sour odor, but he felt sick to his stomach. Paula fumbled in her purse for a tissue for him, hoping that he wasn't going to have a full-blown attack of something. Some others in the room were swooning. One or two got up and fumbled in the dark for the door.

Allen wordlessly hung over Sky and assessed the situation. Then he knelt over and, Paula could swear, put his hand into Sky's belly. He began pulling out what appeared to be a wiggly six-inch silvery fish, cloudy water, and what looked like a liver and intestinal organs. She couldn't be sure that it wasn't some trick, because the room was dim. The chanting grew hypnotic. Allen worked quickly and he seemed to be up to his elbows in Sky's belly. Each time he found something, he pulled it up and out while holding it high for the group to see. The chanting grew louder with each new discovery. Paula worried that Sky wouldn't have any organs left after Allen was done. She had never seen anything even closely approaching this in her life. She was mesmerized and so was Ralph, so much so that his sniffles vanished. Paula's mind wanted a logical explanation, but what she saw defied it.

Paula looked over at Yogianni, who was kneeling in supplication and deep prayer, and despite her envy and wariness of Yogianni, felt genuine compassion for her. Duke, Antonio, Delila, Miracle, Reefdancer and the others appeared grateful for and relieved by the attention and care Sky was receiving.

Then miraculously, Sky started to come to. He moaned but his eyes remained closed. They all breathed a sigh of relief. Sky rested quietly while someone else moved into the center of the circle as Allen first meditated, recouped his energy, and then set to work healing this new person. His protégées carried Sky to the side of the room.

Antonio whispered to the group, "We created a circle of love, a safety net, and now Sky will be okay." He nodded to Allen in thanks.

Finally spent, Allen slumped over. Several women helped him out of the dark room.

"Our Allen has had enough for this evening," the silk-scarved woman said to the group. Slowly, the lights came up so that the room resembled a rosy cabaret, and people shuffled out into the dark balmy night air onto the lawn.

Some stood and watched the waves crash against the rocks and looked up at the starry sky. Others climbed into their vans and drove down the dirt road healed and more enlightened.

"Is he okay? Will he be okay?" Paula whispered.

"We really don't know yet." Duke put his arm around Yogianni's shoulder.

Outside, several minutes later, Ralph found Paula and whispered into her ear, "Won't we be accomplices to a crime if Sky dies?"

18

Reefdancer moved toward Ralph and said in a whisper, "Do you think this guy Frank Fagioli can get the ladies just because he is rich?"

"Why ask me?"

"Well, you seem like you understand a guy like him."

"You mean can you can buy love with money?" Ralph was preoccupied for the moment with an itching sensation on his biceps. He was wondering if it was shingles. "Yeah, it happens."

"Would a woman *really* marry a man just because of his money?" Ralph looked into Reefdancer's eyes and found the essence of innocence looking back at him. *What part of this doesn't he understand*, thought Ralph. Reefdancer and Ralph stood in silence for a moment, staring out into the pitch-blackness of the night. The fragrance of the wild bougainvillea filled the air. The itching had moved down Ralph's arms onto his hands. He stood there scratching. A fear was rising in his belly. The thought crossed his mind that Allen might offer to work on him. He would refuse, at all costs. He couldn't believe that these people would put themselves in the hands of such a quack, but hey, look at where he was right now and how he got here: people who had bad cases of Guru-itis.

Reefdancer said, "Miracle *does* have a career in Colonics. She is known throughout the island for her work. I mean, I hope that I'm not signing my life away tomorrow. I have to work my ass off to make ends meet."

"Does she know that?"

"No, I wanted to create a good impression."

"Is she a shopper?"

"Yes, why?"

"That's always an important sign of your burn-rate. What I mean is, how fast the money is going to evaporate once you pool all your resources?"

Reefdancer chuckled and patted Ralph on the back. "You could say that. Do you have a prenuptial agreement?" asked Ralph.

Ralph had decided to forget the itching and the headache and try to be rational. Maybe it was only the humidity.

"Nope."

Reefdancer felt a cruel whack behind the back of his knees. There had been only a few times in his life when someone had inadvertently penetrated his cloud of denial and gotten through to him. This moment was one of those. It was as if someone had dumped a heavy pack onto his back. In that moment he saw himself as a threadbare indigent sleeping in a worn blanket, his only remaining possession, on the beach. He knew what he had to do, if only he could sustain his resolve.

Just then Paula, Miracle, Delila, Duke and Antonio appeared. "What are you guys doing?" asked Paula.

"I was wondering if you and Paula are joining us at Reefdancer and Miracle's wedding tomorrow?" Antonio asked Ralph.

Ralph and Paula looked at each other. Paula nodded yes. Ralph didn't move his eyes off her.

Ralph desperately needed to slow down the action and signal to Paula that maybe there wouldn't be a wedding, but Reefdancer said nothing. What could Ralph say in that moment? His mind ran through several sentences, words, paragraphs, but they all sounded lame. Will there be a wedding? Reef and I were just deciding that he is getting bamboozled so he's calling it off? Reef, oh Reef, speak up, but Reefdancer remained silent, saving face.

"How's Sky doing?" asked Reefdancer, turning toward the house where Sky lay.

"He's recovering, but he's not out of the woods yet. Allen worked on him again. He's sleeping now. We left Yogianni with him. If things don't improve in the next hour, Yogianni thinks we should take him to the hospital, don't you?" Miracle said.

"There must be a large green plastic bag filled with all his organs by now," whispered Ralph to Paula.

"I didn't know that he couldn't swim," said Delila.

Paula took Ralph by the arm and dragged him off to the side by the pikaki trees. She whispered insistently to him. "Stop it. I want to go to the wedding tomorrow. What's up?"

"I've never been to a personal growth workshop where the leader dies as the grand finale," Ralph hissed. "I wonder if we can get our money back."

"Oh, for God's sake, stop being so dramatic. How mercenary can you be?"

"I didn't know these people forty-eight hours ago, and there may not even be a wedding tomorrow, after my conversation with Reefdancer. Did you know that he doesn't have a pre-nuptial agreement? And I am so pissed that we probably can't even get out of here. We're tied together at the hip, and all our stuff, our airline tickets and our clothes are miles away. I wonder if we'd be invited to the funeral, too? Do you know that I'm coming down with some fatal rash from all this and my head won't quit aching?"

"Well, you think you've got it bad, I still haven't heard a word from my agent about the book. The longer I wait the more worried I am that we won't be able to find a taker."

"I want to know if I still have a job when I return, or if all the young Turks ate me."

"The cell phone transmission isn't really that great here."

"I know. At least it's not your health. If you don't have your health you've got nothing."

"Oh, now we are into our marital one-upmanship?"

They were back in the soup again without warning.

If Paula had known what was just about to blindside her, she wouldn't have flounced away at that moment.

19

Twenty minutes later, sitting by the poolside in the dim light of citronella torches, with the palm trees swaying in the background and the surf crashing nearby, the whole group waited for Yogianni to bring out news of Sky's condition.

"I can't help thinking of those poor people in Massachusetts snowed in that I saw on CNN the other day, while we bask in paradise," said Miracle.

"That is not a very spiritual thing to say," Delila said.

Paula smiled at both of them and breathed in the balmy night air. She felt adrift, disoriented. She had lost her bearings, her Due North, her trim tab. Here anything seemed good as long as it was pleasurable and not too complicated. After all, who could think in ninety-degree humidity? They came here to learn about the G spot: a place of profound pleasure and no pain, a place of enlightenment. Things were not going the way she had planned. She was on tilt. What if Sky got worse? What if he died? Would they be considered accomplices to a murder? She watched Ralph vigorously scratching and rolling around like a dog on the cool grass nearby.

"Really, what happens if Sky doesn't come to? Won't we be responsible?"

Delila was indignant, "Allen is *not* a run-of-the-mill channel, like others. He is a *bona fide* psychic healer. He goes in with hammers, saws, turpentine injections and ammonia enemas. Why, recently I saw people throwing him their car keys to scrape the cornea of the patient's eye. There was absolutely no hygiene and yet the person was healed."

"You mean he injects people with stuff?" said Ralph.

"Yes, and some people even get kicked out!"

"Kicked out? But why?"

"Allen channeled Dr. Botox, and he said to a friend of mine that she didn't believe deeply enough in the process. She was crushed. No one in the community will speak with her now. She was ejected!"

"You mean rejected, don't you, honey?" said Paula.

"Rejected. We thought that she wrecked it for everyone, and Dr. Botox, I mean Allen, you know, threatened to leave."

Reefdancer was still wondering out loud, "Do you think that if you are wealthy enough, you get more women?"

Miracle shot him a menacing glance.

"Still working on that, old pal?" said Ralph sarcastically. His itching was taking on monumental proportions. How could he have so stupidly left his Benadryl in his bag back at the workshop? "Since we have nothing else to do, let's take a poll here." Ralph was trying to take his mind off his latest infliction. He looked around the circle of Miracle, Delila, Paula and the guys.

In that moment everyone seemed relieved to follow his lead and take their mind off Sky's condition.

"Just for fun, let's say that there are three doors, just like the quiz show. And behind each door there is a different man. You get to choose one to marry."

The women's ears perked up. Open for fun, always. Everyone drew up chairs and came closer. Paula had been privy to this behavior before. Ralph fancied himself as a bit of a Maury Povich or Phil Donahue at times. It grew out of his advertising background and focus groups, she had surmised when she first met him.

"Behind door number one we have a wealthy middle-aged man, very generous financially, like Frank Fagioli, but he's never home and he has a cell phone stuck to his ear." Ralph offered a long dramatic pause. "You can buy everything except intimacy."

"Wait, you mean he gives you everything but *sex*?" asked Delila incredulously. She had already chosen when Ralph said the operative word, money, but this last thing he said was causing her doubts. "Well, does he like oral sex?"

Ralph laughed. "Yes, if you don't mind if he's on an international call while you are going down on him. His mind won't be present, but maybe the rest will." Everyone laughed. They were all getting into Ralph. They had never seen this side of him as master of ceremonies.

"He's no good in bed?" asked Miracle.

"I didn't say that," Ralph smiled slyly. "I just said that his libido isn't super-charged and maybe he has a very small pencil holder."

"Is he old and ugly, too?" Miracle asked, considering her choice.

"Does he need a walker? Wouldn't you hate to marry a rich old man who dies on your honeymoon night and his kids contest his will?" Paula said.

"No, he's mobile. He can walk on his own," Ralph played along, trying to answer everyone's concerns.

"Could we revive him with a vibrator?" asked Paula.

"I didn't say he was dead."

The women giggled.

Paula turned towards the women. "You'll never believe this, but my girlfriend Snookie found this gigantic vibrator at Ace Hardware that looked like an electric sledge hammer. She brought it back to school in the dead of winter. All us girlfriends practiced on it, vibrating at one hundred miles an hour, and it practically ripped off our softer organs with its velocity. We were hot then! In my forties, we were at a different life stage, so for my birthday, she bought me one that was smaller, but had many interesting attachments that Ralph and I experimented with. Last year, with our waning libidos, she gave me one for my birthday that went at thirty-three and one third revolutions per minute, like old Perry Como records."

"Speaking of vibrators," continued Ralph, "behind door number two, you have a guy several years younger than you women, who is a great lover. You have many sensuous nights, but he's not a warrior, he's an artist and he can't make a living. But you have great sex with all kinds of vibrators, dildos and Ben Wah Balls. He's his own one-stop shop — sex shop."

"Wow," said Delila.

Everyone began debating but Ralph hushed them. "Wait, there is one more door, ladies. Behind door number three, you have a guy who is very adventurous, he takes you all around the world. He makes an average living, he takes you to romantic places. But he is impotent, although he is very loyal and would never leave you for anyone else."

"Does he get hard, at least?" asked Miracle.

"Yes, but he never comes. You can ride him for hours," said Ralph.

"Well," Miracle said looking at Reefdancer, "at least he comes."

"Well, you know that in Tantric it isn't good to ejaculate often because my Tantric Guru, Dr. Jacobs, said that you only have so much seed to burn, and if you use it all up, you deplete yourself. That's the reason why men die earlier than women," Reefdancer asserted, answering Miracle's look.

"How do you know Dr. Jacobs?" asked Paula.

"He was the one who taught Sky everything he knows."

Paula felt the ripple of shock. She realized that Ralph didn't even know about Dr. Jacobs and she wasn't going to be the one to ever tell him any of the story.

Was there a cultural axis between Marin and Tortola that she was just discovering now? Was that why Dr. Jacobs acted so strangely in the later part of their appointment? She just couldn't reconcile that her gynecologist had been tied into these people and had practiced his craft here.

Ralph stored Reefdancer's comment away to think about later, because everyone was busy debating their choices. The game had taken their minds off Sky's condition.

Above the excitement, Ralph shouted, "Okay, okay, who would you choose?"

"Doesn't every relationship have a kicker, though?" Paula said cynically.

Ralph didn't look at his wife, but her mere presence was heartening. He felt that there was a touch of genius in her ability to navigate the intangible world. She made interesting observations that never failed to astonish him. It was only her lack of softness that failed her. Perhaps it was because of her interfacing with the world of commerce, but he longed for softness in her.

Delila went first. "I'd choose the guy who was rich, and take the lover on the side."

Everyone laughed except Miracle. She gave Delila a sharp look. "How can you say that? I'd choose the great lover. Period," said Miracle, smiling at Reefdancer.

Delila could tell that she had said something to offend Miracle, but she wasn't quite sure what. Could she have said something to betray Miracle and Reefdancer or herself? She wasn't sure. Reefdancer was a good lover, but she wasn't sure that he was as well off as Miracle thought he might be. Didn't she know?

"Can I do this for homework?" said Paula laughingly.

"No really, tell us!" said Antonio. He was curious about Paula. He had never met a woman who traveled in the world of television.

"Well, I really didn't know who Ralph was as a lover when I met him on a commuter plane, I mean, which one of these lovers we are talking about. But I can tell you one thing. I didn't know him all that long before he proposed to me. In fact, we had planned a wedding at the Jersey shore at a fancy hotel, and hired some wonderful musicians to play. We had about one hundred and fifty guests. Just as I was walking down the aisle, out of the bushes comes Ralph's ex-girlfriend! And she was dressed in a wedding gown similar to mine." Paula paused.

The group of women gasped.

"She started screaming that Ralph didn't love me, he loved her, and I was mortified. She began pulling on my dress and before I knew it, we were in the ocean ripping at each other's headdress and clothes. I was so angry at Ralph for not telling me about her, and shocked and angry that this was happening to wreck my wedding."

"What did the guests do?" Miracle asked.

"They were in shock like a bunch of sheep, they moved down to the beach to watch. I was mortified. All I could think of was my parents and my relatives were watching this horror show! I should have known better than to fight with this gal, but she kept pulling on me until we were in the surf. She turned out to be his college sweetheart and felt that she had a claim to him."

"Did she?" Reefdancer asked.

Ralph was laughing one of those sounds some men seem to make when they are caught: a sound that was a cross between a belly chuckle and a croak. It was Ralph who finally answered.

"Well, let's say we kept in touch all these years via letters, but I had no idea that she was 'fatal attraction.' She turned out to be a nut case. Some guests called out the hotel security guards who sped into the ocean with water ski mobiles to break up the fight, but they collided with one another and the ski mobiles flew out of the water."

"Yeah, meanwhile, my gown lay in shambles floating on the surf, but I got a good piece of her," Paula continued. "Some women wedding guests, trying to be helpful, stood at the edge of the surf picking up the remnants of our clothing before they got washed out to sea."

"And the musicians kept playing as if nothing was going on. We can laugh at it now, dear, can't we," said Ralph. "We finally got married quietly several days later at the city hall."

Paula gave him one of those looks with pursed lips and a shaking head.

"Let's just say that it wasn't a shining moment in our relationship life. I really gave Ralph the third degree before we decided to move ahead to city hall."

"Yeah, she asked me about all the other skeletons that were in the closet."

"Aren't you supposed to get all that stuff out before the ceremony and after the first lovemaking session?" Delila asked.

Like most married couples, Paula and Ralph could read each other's non-verbal cues. She could tell that Ralph was really enjoying himself. As long as he did that, he could forget about his aches and pains.

Paula didn't answer, because she wanted to keep a low profile, and didn't want to play her cards too openly. She hoped that she could fly under the radar until this was over. She was still thinking about her disappointment at not getting any phone calls back on the mainland about her book results.

Everyone was enjoying this distraction. So Paula felt comfortable enough after awhile to turn the conversation to herself and the domain of women and their tastes. When Delila spoke, Paula was ready to answer.

"But you still haven't answered the question."

"I guess I'm an old-fashioned gal, I *love* to shop. I'd choose number one."

The women gasped at Paula's honesty. The men shot each other looks. "Look, it's a very primitive instinct to look for protection from a man. What woman doesn't want a man to be the rescuer, and what woman doesn't want a man to be the 'wind beneath her wings?' "

Paula knew that her tough armor was a defense at times. She would relish the day when someone would rescue her and let her kick back and be pampered. She was tired of being a tough-minded businesswoman.

"Hey, I thought you were an independent woman," said Antonio, the gate-keeper who had brought two women.

"Let's just say we women are very complex."

"But these celebrities, for example, women just flock around them, and some of them are pint-size."

"Pint-size in every department?"

"How would I know, but they are short. Some are even unattractive, but women just fall all over them."

"Duh! They have dough. You can be the ugliest guy on the face of the earth, but sit at some bar and hang one hundred dollar bills out your ears, and watch women come flocking," said Delila.

"Wait. How about us women!" Paula shouted. She had the men interested now. "I'm going to give you guys three scenarios. Behind door number one we have a woman who is young, dark, with smooth skin, many curves. She supports herself by selling puka beads on the beach, no, I'm just kidding. She supports herself selling her art, but once she gets married, she falls into her man's arms and makes him support her."

"What's so good about that?" asked Reefdancer.

"Well, she's lovely and a good sex partner, after all."

"If Sky were here, I wonder who he would choose," Delila said.

"Probably all of them!" Reefdancer chuckled.

Miracle jumped up. "I don't want to play this game anymore! Reefdancer, you said that we were going to have our love day before our wedding tomorrow. Besides, we have to prepare!"

Reefdancer looked sheepishly around the group. "I gotta go, guys and gals." He was trying to save face.

Miracle flashed a quick smile at everyone, grabbed Reefdancer's arm and walked him back to the house.

"What was that about?" asked Paula.

"Oh, Reefdancer promised Miracle their love day," said Duke. "Maybe she was afraid it wouldn't happen. After all, the night is almost over."

Antonio was the first to rekindle the discussion. "You ask a very provocative question, Paula dear. I think most men would want a woman to be available to our every desire and need. Wouldn't you agree?" He looked at the remaining men around the table.

Ralph laughed. "Yes, sexual goddess, wife, mother, *au pair*, courtesan and housekeeper, right? Did I cover everything?"

Antonio and Duke shook their heads in violent agreement, while Delila and Paula rolled their eyes in disgust.

About midnight Yogianni found the group still sitting at the pool. "Sky is going to be okay," she said. "He is awake and just ate something." Everyone gave a sigh of relief. Ralph found himself hugging Yogianni as if he had known her all his life. They had all been through something together. He looked into her eyes and saw a tear escape down the side of her cheek.

"Thank you so much for saving his life this morning."

Ralph just held her close and felt her soft, yielding vulnerability. He was turned on.

20

Miracle was relieved with her quick thinking she had dragged Reefdancer away from the pool and all those people to be by themselves. After all, their wedding was the next day, and Miracle had plans for them.

Earlier, she had run out and purchased the special estrogen cream and put it in the right place just as Yogianni had suggested that she do. It was a surefire suggestion to turn up the heat, and heat she felt. All afternoon long she felt the inner fires being stoked through chemistry.

The coverlet was dowsed with coconut and vanilla essence, the aromatherapy sold in Road Town boutiques. She had made a special trip to purchase it.

Now that she had gotten her man, she wanted him to see fireworks the night before the ceremony so that he'd know that he made the right decision. She didn't want him to go to some sleazy bachelor party the night before, with sexy girls jumping out of cakes, and come home drunk. She wanted to stage her own night before the wedding shindig.

Thank goodness she was able to pull him away from that group of people, and Sky was on the mend. Yes, a human but a selfish part of her was grateful for Sky's delivery from the hands of death, or the wedding would have had to be postponed, and she never could have lived with that for one minute.

She put on her sexual costume. She donned the sure-fire method of seduction she had learned at Sky's school: one black garter belt, one pair of stockings, and one black push-up bra. Then she waited for Reefdancer to finish his joint that he always smoked to get him in the mood. This particular afternoon Reefdancer had taken too many tokes, and he was pie-eyed by the time he got into bed with Miracle.

As a sexual marathoner, despite the cannabis, and unlike lesser men on controlled substances, he entered her with no problem.

She was already writhing around with joy because the estrogen cream combined with the heat of Reefdancer's member created the chemistry of explosive sex. Miracle had never experienced such fire and desire before in her life, she was wild with joy, and she wasn't known to not express herself.

A stoned Reefdancer listened as Miracle tried to talk to him about the prenuptial agreement, all the time she was writhing, cooing and sucking in foreplay. She had thought she might have more luck if she caught him with a stoner's mind.

He listened thoughtfully and half-smiling as she prattled on.

Miracle was certain that she was reaching him, and his half-smile was acknowledging her cuteness and effort in all these preparations.

Finally, once there was a moment where Reefdancer could exhale. "I can't do it without the paper. I'll leave it on the dresser for you to sign before tomorrow morning."

He crawled onto her again. He lifted his eyebrows and threw back his head at the banquet before him. He inserted his hard member into her and came quickly. Then he dozed off in a stupor before Miracle gave her usual ohs and ahs.

173

She continued the sex play as he slept, and finally rolled off minutes later. She was still burning with desire, but she decided that she shouldn't wake him. It was going to be a big day tomorrow, and they both should get some sleep.

She threw the thin sheet over them, and locked the sliding screen door. All was silent. The night sky lay like a velvet blanket with twinkling lights of Apple Bay.

He woke suddenly at three in the morning.

"I am paralyzed, I can't feel my penis!" He yelped and jumped out of bed.

She rolled over and put a pillow over her head. She lay naked and the sheet lay on the floor beside the bed. The air smelled so fragrant at that time of the morning, close to heralding a new day in paradise. It was her wedding day.

He held his member as if to warm it and then went running into the bathroom.

She heard the water running in the sink. "What's that, honey?" she asked sleepily

"It's the cold water."

Miracle looked up slowly, still in a haze, and said, "Honey, that was the best sex I ever had."

He yelled back from the bathroom, "What did you do to me? It isn't moving. It stings."

"In what, honey?" she said dreamily.

He stood over the toilet. "I can't even pee. What is happening to me?'

Miracle jumped up out of bed, tousled and spacey from love-making.

"Oh honey, what can I do? What is it?"

"Just leave me alone." He pushed her out of the bathroom and slammed the door.

There his member was hanging, red and swollen, burning and stinging like crazy. He had never felt such pain. Did he all

174

of a sudden get syphilis? Could that happen so rapidly? Was this retribution for all the years of unsafe sex? Was it punishment from too much masturbation as a child? Was his mother right, bless her soul, after all?

Suddenly it dawned on her. He was having a full-blown anxiety attack, but she didn't know how to stop it.

She was standing against a closed door, excluded and exiled. She couldn't make sense of it. In all of their lovemaking, this kind of behavior had never happened before.

"I can't believe we are getting married tomorrow, and now this! That was the worst sex I ever had."

Miracle pressed her ear to the door. She couldn't believe what she had just heard.

"What did you do to me?"

"Nothing, nothing." Large tears welled up in her eyes. She sobbed loudly.

"Is this what it is going to be like after we are married?"

Before she could answer he opened the door and ran past her, grabbing his shoes, underpants, trousers, and tropical shirt as he ran out of the hotel room into the early dawn.

A bewildered Miracle sat at the edge of the bed. Her black garter belt, stockings and bra lay on the floor beside her.

21

The next morning, Delila was sitting in the chair of The Paradise Salon and talking to her new hair stylist. "I'm going to a wedding and I need an incredible haircut."

Fiona, the stylist, had come highly recommended by Yogi-anni, so Delila felt very secure in the plush leather pink seat in the shopping mall.

"Oh, are you going alone, or with someone? Weddings are such a special time to go with your main squeeze. Don't you think?"

Delila noticed that Fiona moved very slowly and deliberately, as if she had been too long on the island and endured too much humidity. This left Delila wondering if she would ever get finished in time to get everything done that day.

Fiona pushed back a skein of her flaming red curly hair that had dropped onto Delila's face during the shampoo.

Eyes closed, Delila shouted up at her above the sound of the water. "My man, Duke, we are going together. Don't you just love weddings?"

Fiona stopped shampooing Delila's hair long enough to look her straight in the eyes. "I am sensing something important here. Is your energy tied up with someone else?"

"Well, Duke, of course!"

One of the blonde-haired stylists leaned over from an adjoining wash-basin at which she was shampooing another woman's hair. "Fiona is a world-class psychic. We are lucky to have her working for us. She told me that my son, who was having trouble in school, had dyspesia."

"No, dyslexia, Irene," Fiona burst in to correct her.

"Well, anyway, I told the teacher in the school." Irene stopped and pointed the shampoo bottle at Delila. "And he was tested and that was it. Now, how could Fiona know all that?"

"I believe that you must follow your destiny or nothing good will happen to you," Fiona lectured as she massaged in the shampoo.

"Gawd, I thought I *was* following my destiny," said Delila.

For awhile, Delila pondered Fiona's comments. She was enjoying the time away from the group and looking forward to the wedding. Fiona towel-dried her hair and was beginning to comb it out, getting ready to cut it. "I don't know who this guy is on a earthly plane, but I know your energy is linked to his energy, and there is definitely a mismatch."

Delila was listening intently as Fiona clipped away and continued talking.

The trouble was, she knew in her gut that Fiona was right. Ever since Duke came home late that night, she was suspicious of his goings and comings. And he came and went more frequently and at odd hours. She was almost tempted to follow him, but only her pride held her in check.

"Yes, I truly believe that bad things happen if your energy is linked to his energy and it's not supposed to be. Especially since I see a sexually blocked man, and you are not. You are definitely not!" Fiona emphasized the point by pointing the scissors in the air as if she were lecturing a college class.

At this point, amidst the roar of blow driers, hair drying machines and other clients' chatter, Delila went into high emotional gear. "He *is* sexually blocked, well, at least with me. He doesn't seem to want lovemaking the way I do. He just hides under the covers, watches the ball games and says he's tired."

"I see that he isn't sexually blocked with other women."

Delila was going through a silent meltdown as she listened. "What do I do?" she finally asked, as she tossed her head around and looked at her new hairdo.

"I see you on a beach."

"Oh great! Where?"

"It's in South Beach."

"Florida?"

"On the Mainland. Yes, but the window of opportunity is very small."

"What?"

"You must hurry. I see a doctor. A medical doctor." Fiona spoke over the sound of her blow dryer. She thought that Delila's hair was turning out great.

"Yes?" Things were looking up for Delila. She could feel it in her soul. The woman knew the Duke was "sexually blocked." That meant to Delila that the woman was the real McCoy psychic.

"You mean he is rich?"

"Yes, he is a rich doctor and he is waiting for you. That is your destiny. You can go now. It is the only way you can unlink from your partner. I've unlinked you psychically to follow your real destiny. I see a brief window of opportunity. But hurry."

Delila paid Fiona and ran out of the shop. She knew what she had to do and she had a great haircut besides. But first she was going to the wedding.

22

The wedding took place on a nearby beach. Ralph, standing in the crowd of three hundred of Miracle and Reefdancer's closest friends, never would have believed what he had gone through over the last twenty-four hours, thanks to his wife. He felt he was part of the family here; but like his birth family, he hadn't chosen them. He longed to escape and be back in the comfort of his home. Maybe he needed to see a lawyer when he got back. He felt frightened at entertaining this thought.

He knew that he was the kind of guy to whom changes come hard. He was most at home with his VCR, his dogs and his television.

"I looove weddings," whispered Paula at his side. She locked her arm around his. "I tell all my girlfriends that weddings are the best place to meet single men. It puts men in the mood, shall we say?"

"Yeah, it hypnotizes them!" Ralph sneered. His rash had disappeared after he had pored over his Merck Manual. He was glad that he had thrown the tissue paper-thin, seven hundred-page manual into his swim bag. The rash was transforming itself into a sinus headache as he watched more and more guests arrive on the small beach. Maybe he had a brain tumor after all. He was used to diagnosing himself and he was becoming certain of the tumor theory after pouring over page 1123 in Merck.

An easel and cardboard sign were set up to announce the private party that directed the way to the "Celebration of Reefdancer and Miracle: his beloved."

A scantily clad woman in her twenties was handing out garlands of pikaki flowers to the male guests in their fifties and sixties in flowered shirts and baggy shorts. They wore no shoes. Gold chains, nose rings, bare feet and balding heads with ponytails were the fashion. The woman kissed the female guests carefully on either side of their cheeks, French style, out of respect for their carefully made-up faces.

"Is this where all the trophy wives end up with their brain-deteriorated husbands?" asked Paula, holding on tightly to Ralph.

"Yes, honey, after the first face lift. You know it's a cold cruel world out there," Ralph joked.

Paula took the garland and wrapped the pikaki flowers around her neck. "I guess the women's liberation movement hasn't made it to this island yet."

Near the water's edge, an eight-piece band was playing a Jamaican version of "Ave Maria," complete with bongo drums and wooden sticks. Someone had dragged a huge Korg synthesizer and speakers onto the sand. "Ave Maria" segued into "The Hawaiian Wedding Song" and then the Don Ho favorites.

A buzzing overhead caused Ralph to glance up. He saw two light planes with banners tailing after them advertising free sun tan lotion in Long Bay. But he was distracted just then as Yogianni was blowing soap bubbles at him.

"How's Sky?" Ralph asked.

"Sky is over there lying on the beach and preparing. He's on the mend, thanks to your help yesterday. He'll be officiating."

Ralph made a mental note to head in that direction when the smooth strong voice of Sky boomed through the speaker system.

"I don't know what I can ever do to thank you," Yogianni said seductively.

Ralph felt his insides flip-flop. He didn't know if it was indigestion or lust.

"I invite all of the guests to convene near the canopy and we shall begin this celebration with a wonderful guy and a wonderful gal with all the ingredients of a perfect day."

Young girls danced ahead, blowing bubble trails to lead people down to the canopy filled with flowers at the water's edge.

Flute and guitar now filled the air. The calm water lapped against the shore. Two small children, guided by a man in a top hat, rolled out a red carpet on the sand and off to the side. A friend of the wedding couple blew several long hollow sounds on a ceremonial conch shell to convene the group.

The guests grew silent when suddenly on the horizon a canoe appeared with the wedding party. As they rowed closer to the shore, Pachebel's "Canon" came on the speakers.

Miracle, transformed by flowers, in a white off-the-shoulder satin dress, crinoline skirt, cinched waist and lots of makeup appeared rising out of the boat on to the shore. Everyone gasped. There she stood more beautiful than anyone had ever seen her. She had transformed herself into a portrait of a Caribbean beauty.

"She looks radiant," said Delila.

"What happens now?" Duke said loudly. "Where is the groom?"

The wedding party languished. Nothing was happening. The guests began milling around, whispering and speculating on what had happened.

Delila grasped Duke's arm tightly and said, "I think they had a fight last night about the prenuptial agreement. Miracle refused to sign anything. She called me in the early morning crying. I told her to go through with it and deal with it afterwards, and Reefdancer, who loves a good party, would cave in and show up. He has more to lose. I just didn't think he would pull this."

"Yeah, women can really suck you in and wind you around their little fingers and leave you penniless, eh Delila?" Duke said.

"Oh, shut up, Duke," said Delila as she flounced off into the crowd.

Duke turned to Ralph. "Oh, don't worry. Maybe Reefdancer got that Miracle is a professional."

"A professional what?" asked Ralph.

"A professional gold digger," continued Duke. "My Delila wrote the book on gold digging. She's been married five times and each time she's taken her husband to the cleaners. Last time she blew through four million dollars in two years."

"My gawd, how?" Paula was incredulous.

"She gave his money to a financial guy named Johnny Freedom who invested it in an off shore scam in the Cayman Islands. Her ex-husband had to move into a retirement home with his brother in Arizona to finally make ends meet.

"You had me fooled, I thought you two were an item." Ralph held up his index and middle finger indicating closeness.

"Were is the operative word," said Duke.

Antonio piped up, "Here in the islands relationships change rapidly! People come to the island and want to learn everything Caribbean. They try to act just like the natives. You know, in matters of love and many wives, ha ha."

Paula's head was spinning with confusion at the velocity of the changes in relationships within the last forty-eight hours. She felt like a foot-dragging Neanderthal in her marriage to

Ralph, but was also glad that theirs was a marriage that was lasting.

"Yeah, at first, when Miracle was planning the wedding, she and Reefdancer were knocking themselves out taping dolphin sounds. They wanted their wedding to have real dolphin music, but it was too hard. Reefdancer almost drowned trying to get a good dolphin sound. So they began imitating dolphins and recording it at a musician friend's house. But the musician's wife kicked them out when their moaning and groaning kept her kids awake."

Paula was overhearing a conversation close by. "Was that the broad who wouldn't let her husband go to our men's group or play in the wedding band because they didn't want her to sing?"

"No, but I know that one. She has these big bazookas, silicon breasts, and they are leaking. It's become her life mission to expose the medical community about it," laughed Duke.

At that moment they were interrupted by Sky, who appeared well enough to officiate at the wedding but was still helped by several women to the podium. "It is with great difficulty that I must tell you our wedding has been postponed . . ."

Just as the news was spreading and the crowd was murmuring about this mishap, they heard the sound of hooves and the earth rumbling near the entrance to the beach. The group turned almost as one. Galloping across the beach was a white stallion, with a huge green tea garland around its neck, decked out in a red blanket. Reefdancer was riding bareback towards Miracle. Everyone let out a gasp and drew back instinctively to make room for the massive horse and rider. Reefdancer came to a sudden halt, threw up mounds of sand and dust, and disembarked before his lovely bride.

Paula was breathless. Miracle, despite a dusty gown, was grinning ear to ear.

"This is so romantic," Paula gasped, looking toward Ralph.

"I can't stand it," Ralph said. "At least he didn't have to rent a hotel ballroom. He got off cheap using the beach."

Paula thought about her own wedding mishap and fantasized at that moment about renewing her vows in a dramatic ceremony like this one with Ralph and her new set of friends. She noticed that she was moving towards him emotionally, unlike the way she felt several days ago, on her arrival. But maybe the wedding was just putting her in an unusually romantic mood.

To Ralph, the ceremony seemed endless as he stood outside the canopy under the hot sun. He was thinking that his brain tumor was growing with every passing moment.

Everyone was whispering superlatives about the day and the couple. Shalimar, an ex-Brooklyn refugee and part-time night club singer, sang her Jamaican-style chants; Kamie, a forgotten 'sixties rock star sang her ex-hit single; Matanli, a now graying and once famous folk singer, made up a song on the spot about the couple, and the crowd was prompted to sing the chorus. A moon-faced pastor and his wife, old Berkeley hippies and founders of a famous organization of healing in Northern Oregon, came up to bless the couple with white light. Everyone was asked to 'Om' for several minutes non-stop.

After other spontaneous presentations, Zoomie, a local friend to all black rap artists read his unpublished sonnet, *Black-Dog-White*. Then the couple was ready to take their vows.

Miracle and Reefdancer took each other's hands and gazed into each other's eyes. Because they were stoned to the bone, the moon-faced pastor smiled ear-to-ear and said all the parts of the ceremony, even the 'I do's', which they mouthed a little above a whisper. Then he pronounced them man and wife.

A roar went up among the crowd as Reefdancer swooped Miracle into his arms and lifted her, despite the fact that he was swaying with the load. His horse lurched around, snorting and stamping, until Reefdancer managed to set Miracle's girth securely astride his stallion.

They galloped off together, both threatening to slide off at any moment. Then they galloped back.

"Just like Reefdancer, with a flair," sighed Yogianni. There was a sea of sighing women, like a wave. Miracle surely was the envy of every woman at the wedding that day.

Paula reflected on her own fiasco of a wedding. She longed for what she just saw. She would renew her vows with Ralph when they went back to Marin. She knew of a little gazebo in Tiburon right at the edge of the water that would be perfect. She would tell Ralph about it this evening when they were alone.

Ralph stood by her side unimpressed. He whispered, "I hope he remembered to put the horses at the end of the parade, or the flower girls will be stepping on horse patties."

Paula just shook her head at him.

The band struck up the music, tables with food appeared in the back, champagne began to flow, and some of the guests moved onto the dance floor. Paula saw Fawn, the woman with the rooster. She was doing a belly dance on the sidelines of the dance floor. Duke stood several feet from her. Fawn's arms were undulating in Duke's direction and she stared into Duke's love-filled eyes.

Delila appeared at Paula's side.

"There is a psychic here named Fiona and she read my mind. She is also a great hair stylist." Delila shook her head so that her blonde locks danced around her shoulders to illustrate the point. "She said that if I take a plane to South Beach in the next forty-eight hours and if I drive to the beach, I'll meet a man."

"On the beach?"

"Yeah, and he'll be wealthy and want to marry me."

"Do you believe her?"

"Oh, she is very good," Delila said. They both stood and watched Fawn's undulations for several minutes, unnoticed in the throngs of guests.

"What about Duke?" asked Paula.

"Oh, Duke," said Delila. "He can do what he wants for all I care." With that she turned on her heel toward the bar to refill her champagne glass.

Once Delila had another glass of bubbly to fortify her, she stomped up and confronted Duke directly. She pulled him aside. "I got to talk to you about something right now," she said close to his face. "Who do you think you are dancing with? I thought you came with me."

He could tell she was somewhat intoxicated, and he hated her like that. "I did, but can't I dance with another woman, for heaven sakes? We're not tied together at the hip, are we?"

Delila was getting up more courage. The drinks, the support and acknowledgment of Fiona had helped with her cause. "I want to know why you don't want to have sex with me as often?"

"Do we have to discuss that here and now? I mean, can't it wait?"

"No, I want to know who she is." Delila was pointing straight at Fawn.

"Oh, that's Fawn. You must know her. She lives near where I go to work."

"You don't have an office, you work on the beach."

"Well, that's what I mean."

"Are you sleeping with her?"

Duke, not a very good liar, and an honest man by nature, looked at her in a pleading way.

"Not now, Delila. Not here."

"What? How could you? She is homeless. You slept with a homeless person. How disgusting!"

Delila felt confused. Duke hadn't even refuted his sin. He just stood there like a big jerk with a shamed look on his red face. Wasn't she more attractive and well-endowed? Fawn was dirty, homeless, without the energy and vitality that Delila had. What could he possibly find attractive about her?

"Er, she . . ." Duke began the long spiral downward in an admission of guilt, while he thought that he was bailing himself out. "She needed help and I thought that I could help her. She is a lovely person."

"She is homeless."

"What does being homeless have to do with it? If you mean that she doesn't have money, neither do I. You went through it!"

"Oh, so that's the deal. Well, I'm fed up. Everyone is gossiping about me behind my back, and I can't live with that. My hairdresser, a top-level psychic, told me about you. She said we shouldn't be energetically linked, so I am unlinking myself from you right now. You are free to go! Go to the homeless person. My things will be cleared out by morning!"

Duke stood there, stunned, as Delila flounced off.

Just then, Zoomie, the self-proclaimed award-winning sonnet poet of the twentieth century, called the crowd together. "I want to make a toast, because I am Reefdancer's longest and best friend." His voice boomed over the speaker system. "A toast to the happy couple. They are perfectimundo for each other. This dudo-rama has been married before and doesn't he put on a fabulous wedding? A toast to Reefdancer.

"I am proud to say," Zoomie continued, "that I was at his last wedding which took place on a yacht in the Gulf of Mexico. Although that marriage lasted about three days, it was fabulous. An extravaganza."

"Is this guy high or drunk?" Paula turned toward Ralph.

"I think he is drunk, but honest."

"Everything was fun until the back of the yacht caught on fire from the barbeque in the front," Zoomie said. "I was on shore getting some more booze. I looked out the window on the sixth floor of the hotel, and I saw guests jumping off the yacht in their wedding clothes and stoned to the gills. I'm glad that we can celebrate on land this time with Reef-dancer and his beloved. Long may he reign."

He lifted his glass. Everyone raised their champagne glasses in a toast.

"Peace, love, joy. Aloha spirit fills our hearts. We call our planet Earth and ask it to bless this beloved couple." He ended and disappeared from the microphone.

"That's Zoomie," laughed Antonio. Chakra and Moon Dancer had their arms around Antonio's waist.

The music started up again. Paula left Ralph's side and mingled with strangers and her new friends. She drank, danced, and felt free for the first time since the Sky crisis. The hot sand warmed her feet, and her body was drenched in sun. She could feel her cells storing up energy for when she had to go back to the mainland. Their time was almost over. She wandered off down the beach to be alone and look out at the ocean.

Later, when the sun disappeared over the horizon in a red ball, everyone stopped to appreciate the flaming finale. They moved toward the person they came with. The crowd had thinned out. The caterers were breaking down the tables and hauling the trash off the beach. The sun felt cool on the sand beneath her feet. After the party, Reefdancer and Miracle had gone off to a nearby hotel to honeymoon for an evening. She returned and looked around, but Ralph was nowhere to be found.

Paula wandered around the remaining guests as the wedding wound down. Duke asked her, "Where is Ralph?"

"I don't know." Paula was embarrassed that she couldn't locate her husband.

"Maybe he just took a walk down the beach. I'll take you back to the workshop, if you like. You can wait for him there. He can catch a ride with someone else."

Paula hadn't seen Ralph on her walk on the beach, and she couldn't imagine leaving without Ralph, but soon it grew dark. She finally got in Duke's car and let him take her back.

Ralph never showed up that evening. There were his clothes, his cell phone, his papers and his bag with all his pills where he had left them in the room. She picked up her cell phone. Who could she call? Who did she know on the island besides this group of people? She didn't want to put a damper on the wedding day. Maybe he was trying to prove something to her. Paula tried calling her agent again to take her mind off his absence. Maybe she had some news about her book sale. The phone registered a no-transmission signal before she slammed it down and threw herself onto the bed. She was certain that her marriage was over. She was hanging on by her fingernails. She was acutely aware that she had no more tools to cope with this than a child, despite years of skepticism as an adult. Suddenly, she had a small epiphany that her Charlton Heston-God-look-alike was strongly affiliated with the National Rifle Association. Nevertheless, "Oh God-help-shit-help" — she repeated her invocation mindlessly. At that moment, God felt like a figment of her imagination.

23

It was the last day of the workshop. Paula was sitting alone in the group room as couples filed in, some hung-over from the wedding. After she exchanged the standard, weather-based pleasantries, she actually noticed that the weather had changed during the early morning. There was a sweet, steamy smell of damp clothes and moldy rugs in the room. This felt like the sub-tropical climate at its worst. She tried to soldier on.

"I can count on one hand the nights I've slept alone in all the years we've been married. He never came home last night," she moaned.

By this time the women tended to the opinion that Paula was "stuck up," while the men favored the theory that she was "cold." Sky, the acknowledged expert on such matters, observed on more than one occasion to Yogianni that "there was nothing wrong with her that a good boning wouldn't cure."

Delila, seated next to her, patted her arm and consoled her. After she had made the quotidian chit-chat, she put her arm around her, because she felt Paula's vulnerability for the first time. "I can't believe he ran off with Yogianni," Delila whispered conspiratorially.

"Delila, he never would do a thing like that. I know him better than you do."

"Well, I hope you are right. I won't say anything to anybody."

But Paula wondered. She felt her mind folding in over itself and this made her very uneasy. She knew that she and Ralph hadn't exactly been getting along these last few days.

"What do you mean?"

"Well, I know Yogianni and she can be a real snake. Fawn didn't become a bag lady without Yogianni just moving in on her territory, you know."

"Oh-my-god!" Paula gasped. "Could it be?"

When she got back, she looked through Ralph's stuff. He never went anywhere without his vitamins, mineral, anti-oxidants and power bars. His Merck Manual and his dop bag, filled with rows of pills for every occasion, were usually lined up neatly on the bureau. The Merck Manual was gone.

When he hadn't appeared by mid-morning, Paula thought of calling the police and reporting Ralph's disappearance. She blanched when she imagined the headlines of *The Tortola Times*, much less the *San Francisco Chronicle*. It might even make the *Marin Independent Journal*. She decided that she could wait a little longer before sheer terror set in. She was sure that Ralph must have some plausible explanation. He had come home late before. He had never been away all night; well, except the time he got drunk with his friends at a male bonding Shaman drumming party in Fairfax. But that was different. Maybe he met someone he knew. He *was* a real schmoozer. But he owed her an explanation! She was getting embarrassed about this whole affair, these people and this whole episode. She blamed herself. She had used some more poor judgment, she thought.

"I'm sure he has a good reason," Paula said, saving face.

"Alibi, he'll give you an alibi," Delila whispered to her. "They all have alibis."

Paula thought that Delila had been reading her mind.

At the break, Antonio was expounding the virtues of relaxation and ejaculation. "I found that mine works without help, if I make time for it."

Duke laughed, "Big deal, I can do it forever if I have two women helping me, like you."

Paula could see that Antonio sulked for a while with hurt feelings. Chakra and Moon Dancer tried to comfort him by rubbing his head.

Finally, Antonio turned to Paula. "Where's Ralph this morning? Too much wedding?"

That's when Paula spilled the beans. Antonio had been so kind to her these last few days, and she really was so ashamed of Ralph's disappearance with no explanation. She couldn't save face anymore to anyone.

"I don't know where Ralph is," she blurted out to the group.

"See!" Delila stated dramatically.

"Let's just get started, everything will sort itself out!" Sky said, trying to get the group's attention away from her. He didn't seem too concerned about Ralph.

Sky quickly gathered his followers together to get the morning's final demonstration going. "We are going to discuss and demonstrate the male G spot. Yes, men have G spots also."

He took out several little plush puppets made of soft silk and various shades of flesh-colored velour. He explained that his Tantric goddesses had gotten together several months before and sewed some very special things for the workshop. They dedicated themselves to making these very detailed and anatomically correct replicas of the male genitalia. They were complete in every aspect. One had only to put on the flesh-colored velour five-fingered glove. In the center of the glove rose a coral-colored circumcised penis. "It is for demonstration purposes only. Rather than use the real thing, which causes some embarrassment to some of the ladies, we now use these puppets. Multi-orgasmic lovemaking allows men and women to harmonize their often different sexual rhythms and desires," Sky pontificated. "The male yang energy can be explosive, and can ignite very quickly. Women must spread this energy out and help the man control his ejaculation."

He demonstrated this by cradling the velour dummy hand, like a Fabergé egg, and working upward strokes on the plush puppet's penis.

"Let the ladies try this first. Men already know how this works."

A murmur erupted from the crowd of men who might have thought for a moment that Sky was talking about male masturbation.

"The internal G spot can be stimulated through the anus." With this, Sky took the velour puppet hand and plunged the index finger deep into the skin-colored silk anus, a special tunnel sewn in toward the opening of the glove. "Of course you would use lubricant, girls," he added.

Suddenly, he pulled out a red satin gum drop-looking object and held it up high. It was a kidney bean. "See this treasure? Let's imagine that this is the male G spot, when in actuality it is the inner upside wall of the anus. You really would never find this in a male anus unless the guy put it there himself." He chuckled with all the guys at the thought.

"Why don't you give a demo, like you did with Yogianni?" Paula shouted out. She was feeling very belligerent this morning. Somehow she held Sky responsible for what was happening. She knew she was acting irrational, but she didn't care.

If Sky and Yogianni weren't leading this workshop, Yogianni may have gone off with Ralph. She knew she was really losing her self-control now, but she didn't care anymore.

"Darling, I don't think the men in the room would appreciate the demonstration." Sky was holding in his irritability. It seemed like they both were on edge with both partners gone.

Sky turned his back to her and went on.

"Now for homework this afternoon, I'd like you to try experimenting with your partner in your cabin."

Sky had cut the lecture short and dismissed everyone. He figured that if he gave his followers homework, he could look for Yogianni. She was embarrassing him. He was certain it was her way of getting back at him. Maybe she was upset about his Autonomy Day and his sexual behavior, but she would never have the nerve to approach him straight on. He had learned that was just the way she was.

He usually did a physical diagram on the board. He would never embarrass himself and other men in the room by doing a real demonstration. He knew that this could get him in real trouble. He knew that he was going through the motions this morning. Others noticed how distracted he was.

Meanwhile, Paula's mind was going wild. Her thoughts went to Ralph's safety. Maybe she should call all the clinics and hospitals. Maybe he tried to come back late last night and the car he was in overturned in a ditch or worse, went off the sheer edge of the road. She didn't give a damn about the male G spot. She wanted her Ralph. Would he be found off in the shrubs somewhere, dead from a heart attack or a stroke? If he didn't appear soon, she would have to pull together a plan and take action. Everyone was being so blasé about it all, as if it were a natural occurrence here. As she was sure it was. Was she being paranoid in thinking that Ralph was really off with

Yogianni, as Delila was so sure was the case? Her Ralph? Was it possible? He had always seemed so faithful. Maybe he was just getting even. Maybe she should check the airlines. Maybe he took a flight home without her, but Yogianni was missing also. Her mind was running the show, so she decided to do what she did whenever she felt overwhelmed. She took out a pad and pencil and began making a list. Lists usually calmed her down.

Sky looked over to see Paula writing furiously and assumed he had squashed any brewing rebellion in the room. He smiled.

First on Paula's list was to take her mind off Ralph and call her agent again. She dialed her agent, Diana Drew. Once again, there was no transmission on this end of the island. Even if she sold her book, she'd have no one to celebrate with. The wind beneath her wings was gone, maybe with another woman. She should have known all along and not let Yogianni into her bedroom the first night. What good was celebrity if she couldn't celebrate with the man she loved?

She tried Snookie McGants' number. The phone rang four times and then the cell transmission began breaking up. Paula left a message on her answering machine just in case. "Hey Snookie, this is Paula. I called to tell you about our time here. You can't reach me here, but we'll be heading home soon. I have so much to tell you that you would find very interesting! I owe you one for Dr. Jacobs!"

She hung up feeling even lonelier for making the call. This was one of those moments that she couldn't escape with activity and friends, as much as she might try. She had to surrender to her emotions and what she felt was the pain of separation from Ralph, perhaps forever.

Even after Sky disbanded the group for the morning session, she couldn't bring herself to talk to him because she didn't want to admit what might be happening. Yet, it was true that Yogianni had come to the room. How could she have been so stupid with her husband? She realized how much she had taken him for granted in coming on this trip. She never would have surprised him with coming here if she had used her head.

Just find him, she thought. It was one of those times she hated. Just hated. Whenever she got this way she felt like a piece of her heart was missing until Ralph came back.

The sun was shining, the palm trees continued to sway, the ocean smell was caught up in the wind and gentle breezes. All like the post card, but something had changed in her. This place wasn't paradise. It was just a rock out in the middle of the Caribbean without Ralph.

During lunch, just as her anxiety reached a fevered pitch, and she was ready to swing into action, Ralph walked through the door of the dining hall.

24

He walked in alone. She saw him first. She trembled with gratitude and self-loathing. Wasn't she the one who had fantasized about leaving him, about divorce? Wasn't she the one who had manipulated him into this, like all the other controlling, willful things she had done in the past in the name of their relationship: selfish and self-centered. Her mother was right, when you don't have kids, you don't know what it is to sacrifice. Self-absorption funneled exactingly into her career, her book, her needs for recognition and her ambition.

He was so important to her, like the air she breathed, the water she drank or the credit card she used. He was the biggest chunk in her pie chart of priorities. To think she almost lost him. She had wanted to change him and not to accept the relationship as it was. She had nearly blown it.

Why, he's even sauntering, Paula thought. He looked clean-shaven, rested and cheerful. Sky was the first to greet him. She could tell that he was trying to act very casual about seeing Ralph.

"Yeh man, how'zit going? We missed you this morning."

Ralph smiled and slapped Sky's arm.

"How you feeling?" Sky asked.

"Great, really great."

"We were worried about you. I never thanked you for the assist in the ocean."

"That's okay. No problem. Nice wedding yesterday."

"No, really man, you saved my life. I don't know what I would have done. I should have told everyone that I couldn't swim. I just was being stupid, I guess. Really, thanks!"

"It's okay, it's okay," Ralph said.

"You seen Yogianni today?"

"Nope. She's gone?"

"Yup. I thought she was with you."

"Nope, haven't seen her."

Paula rushed over to Ralph and gave him a big hug. She felt herself take a breath for the first time in twelve hours or more.

"Where were you?" she hissed. Now she was angry. She had rights as a wife and she was going to get to the bottom of this as quickly as possible.

"I thought I had a brain tumor, so I got myself to the emergency room of the Tortola hospital."

"Why the *hell* didn't you tell me where you were going?"

"I didn't see you. I was freaked out and upset. I guess you couldn't see that. You were having too much fun."

"I thought you ran off with Yogianni."

"Oh, right. Maybe I would have if I didn't have a brain tumor."

Then it dawned on Paula, there might really be something wrong with Ralph. Even hypochondriacs get sick for real.

"Well, *do* you have something I should know about?" Paula asked sincerely.

"I got checked out and I'm okay. The doctors call this vacation decompression. They say that sometimes when you work really hard and then you stop working, that's when you get symptoms, or worse, that's when you get sick."

"Oh," Paula said, honestly relieved. Ralph having a fatal illness was one step less than him being dead. But he was neither.

"So I just got symptoms. I'm really okay."

"Then where is Yogianni?" piped up Delila who saw the reunion happening. She was annoyed that her fantasy of Ralph and Yogianni going off together hadn't materialized.

"I told Sky, Delila, I just don't know. I didn't know until this minute that she was even missing. But I will tell you one thing, I'd hate to have to do what she is doing."

"What do you mean?" asked Duke.

"While I was sitting in the emergency room away from this place, I really had time to think about all that has happened. I realized that I needed to take a stand in order to feel good about myself. You guys have been very openhearted with me, but I can't believe that I have spent the last several days in this foolishness. Maybe I am cynical or skeptical about your sexual spirituality, but I never fell for this enlightenment stuff, any of it. I gotta be real. I gotta be me."

"Yeah, real is good," said Sky, a little dubiously.

"No, listen Sky, he has something important to say." Antonio reached out and put his arm on Ralph's shoulder.

"You think you have a monopoly on enlightenment," said Ralph. "You act like you've been to the mountain and I haven't. Aren't you the least bit curious about me? What excites me? What I'm interested in? Can you get out from behind your game?"

"Sure, man," said Sky sheepishly.

"I temper my spiritualism with practicality. Somehow, I believe that our flaws, jealousies and anger, are there for a reason. Gurus and workshop leaders hardly ever discuss this. Do all the people on this island only show the bright, optimistic, candy-coated side? You can't just stay in the light all the time.

Oh yes, you can, you can hide there hundreds of miles away from anywhere. Some people may come here to hide. Somehow, from their actions, I can't help but know that their dark, raw side is seething beneath the surface."

"I can't believe you are saying this," said Delila. "That's exactly how I've been feeling all along, but I just couldn't put words to it. That's why I'm going to leave the island, and Duke can belly-dance with Fawn all he wants!"

"Oh, shut up, Delila," shouted Duke.

Ralph went on as if Delila had not said anything. "These last few days have been a distraction of experiences, like a brightly lit carnival of super health, perfect love, universal peace, abundance and limitless sex. I mean, there is no such thing as limited resources here. I can't believe it. If I haven't experienced an unlimited high of personal comfort and universal consciousness, then I am promised that I soon will, right after this next group hug, or group trip. And I'm sick of it!"

"Ralph, I think you have Tourette Syndrome," Paula said.

"What's that?" Delila asked.

"It's when you can't stop saying awful things about people right in front of them. Ralph knows what I mean."

"No, let him finish," said Sky. "He has a right to his opinion."

Ralph was just getting started now.

"The real truth is that we age, get sick and die; we hate each other; we get tired of each other; we make war and half the world lives in abject poverty. You all just have the luxury to contemplate your sexual navels in a beautiful setting. Lucky you. Too bad you believe the crap you feed yourselves. Every other person here has a bad case of Guru-itis."

Sky got red.

Delila looked at Sky and silently pointed her finger at him. Ralph continued, "If you told the truth, you'd have to admit the jealousy, envy and greed we have all felt at one time or another this weekend and often. People rarely reach sexual enlightenment on one weekend. This workshop looks to me like a means to help everyone find ever-loftier rationalizations for maintaining their self-absorption. I'm more interested in people whose spirituality is just there unself-consciously. I'd rather have a wordless experience with an average guy on the commuter bus than the latest self-proclaimed wise man or woman."

"Man, you are so right on," said Duke. He put his arm around Ralph.

"Glad you're back, guy," said Sky magnanimously.

Ralph took a deep breath. He looked around. He had actually come to like Sky. He really liked all these people in a strange way. They were playful, untouched and infantile. He wanted to go home.

"Hey man, let's have a group hug. You can have your opinion, but don't be imprisoned by it. Live and let live, right, guys?" said Sky. "I always say believing is seeing. Everything is perfect the way it is. You can't change anybody."

Without another word, Paula, Ralph, Sky, Antonio, Chakra and Moon Dancer, Delila and Duke gave each other a group squeeze. They even put Ralph in the middle. He had tears in his eyes.

25

"You certainly had me worried," said Paula as she kicked off her shoes and climbed into their hanging bed that night.

"I didn't mean to worry you, I just thought that I was dying and I'd do what any man would do when he felt like he was dying, check himself into the nearest emergency room."

"Why didn't you find me and tell me?"

"I couldn't, I was feeling awful. I wasn't thinking clearly."

"Are you sure you weren't with Yogianni?"

"Oh c'mon."

"What are you doing?" asked Paula as she saw Ralph spreading the blanket and sheets out on the floor at the side of the bed.

"I am sleeping on the floor, what does it look like I'm doing."

Paula slithered on her belly across the sheets and peered over the side of the mattress.

"Is there room for one more down there?"

"Sure, if you don't mind the wood floor. I just need it for my back tonight."

Ralph turned off the lights and lay quietly looking up at the ceiling.

"You know, you missed the homework of finding the male G spot, do you want me to fill you in?" asked Paula. There was a long silence as she peered into the darkness. Only the crickets outside could be heard.

"You can have the night off from this assignment."

Another long silence ensued.

Then Ralph said, "Can I substitute something else for your investigation into my G spot? You have proven that you have keen sexual abilities, but I don't want a proctology exam tonight."

"You mean you want to trade your Phil Rizutto baseball card for something?"

"Yeah, how about my Ted Williams card?" Ralph said laughingly.

"Oh, okay, what you want?"

"If you want to pleasure me, you can rub my chest a little."

"This feels like we are camping out," said Paula, as she dropped down beside him and began to rub his chest. She was glad to scrunch around his hair, then make little circles with her hand on his hairy chest, and smell him again.

"You know, I really learned a lot from these several days, and I am glad you made me come, after all," Ralph said.

"Oh, you are? May I ask what it is you learned? I've learned a lot. What have *you* learned, Ralph?"

"I learned that you have a very complex operation going on down there, but I've learned how to hotwire it."

"Oh, yeah? I bet you still don't have a clue!"

"I love you," he said.

"That's the way I feel about you."

"How? Explain it to me."

"Well, there's a deep space that you occupy between my heart and my stomach." She pointed to her chest bone and her stomach.

He was quick to laugh.

"Are you sure it's not indigestion?"

"No." She wanted to be clearer in her thoughts. "It's a place where when you were gone it was empty and I could feel it strongly vacant, like a hunger or a thirst. But when you came back and we're together now, clicking along, it feels full again. I can tell you everything and you listen to the broken parts. Maybe you're not so good in home improvement, fixing doorknobs and locating the circuit breaker when the lights go out, but you are my healer man. You listen and respond in such a way that I know you've been lost like me, deep within the same wilderness, and you found the same tree, sat beneath it and cried your eyes out about the same things. I guess I just feel better when I'm with you. I didn't know that before this trip."

Ralph rolled over, and accepting the bet, put his hand exactly on the right spot. It felt warm and wet.

Paula, amazed at his accuracy, began moaning with pleasure in record time. She reached over and took hold of Ralph's versatile protuberance, and ever so lightly maneuvered it inside of her.

Little did she know that once again, Ralph had just lucked out with the accuracy of his slow hand. It had been a long shot finding the ever-elusive spot, but Ralph was born under a lucky star.

Much later, after they had sweated, groaned, writhed and pushed the blankets into a rope entangled at the end of the bed, Paula and Ralph sprawled out on their backs, satisfied and happy, replete and peaceful.

Paula wrapped her arms around him as he rolled over and puffed up his pillow. She rested her head on his hard chest. It was their favorite position, a variation of spoon-style, and they slept that way through their last night.

As they drove to the airport, they encountered a traffic jam on Town Road, two miles from the airport.

"What if we don't make this flight?"

"Who would have ever expected a traffic jam and gridlock in paradise?"

Paula laughed at the word paradise. Since the time they had arrived, it had taken on a new meaning. Even paradise could be hard-duty if your partner was missing.

At the next red light, Paula spotted Delila in the car alongside them. Ralph rolled down the window. He yelled across the passenger seat, "Where are you headed?" Then he spotted Yogianni seated next to Delila.

"I'm going to South Beach to meet a rich guy. I'm following the psychic's advice. Yogianni is coming with me. I'm dropping her off in Marin."

Yogianni smiled and waved to Paula and Ralph.

"Where were you yesterday?" yelled Paula, but before Yogianni could answer, the light changed. Delila went speeding off. Ralph and Paula never got a chance to catch up to them again.

"With this traffic, we'll probably miss our plane," Paula said.

"Paula, will you stop worrying. You're giving me a migraine."

"I wish you'd stop belly-aching about your health!"

"I would if you'd stop worrying about things that don't happen. We have plenty of time, now just cool it Have you ever known me to be late for a flight? I've always gotten us there on time."

"You know, this vacation has taught me that we need some rules when we have to go on trips together, like don't belly-ache or talk about your symptoms."

"I only belly-ache when you start worrying unnecessarily."

"We could call them, 'Rules For The Road'." Paula grabbed a piece of paper and began making a list. "Number one is no belly-aching."

"Number two is no worrying about future things. Some of your fondest projections never actually happen, honey."

"Okay, number three is no rehashing each other's past mistakes."

"Wait, I need a bail-out clause."

"Why?"

"What if I am driving and I start belly-aching because I really *am* sick? What if I'm really having a heart attack? Should I just keep my mouth shut, open the door and fall out of the car silently, rather than break our new rules? I want an over-ride clause."

Paula was busily jotting down the rules on the pad she always kept in her purse. "Okay." She read back the list. "Let's keep it under the visor." She reached up and tucked it in there. When she flipped the visor, the list popped into her lap. They both laughed.

"I can't forget to take it with me when we turn in the car. Although, I'm sure the next couple could use these as well."

They sat in an awkward silence for a long time. The traffic was at a standstill; slowly it began to move.

Ralph spoke first. "I guess we have nothing to talk about any more."

Paula turned toward Ralph. "I guess without our resentments, we have no glue to keep us together."

They both giggled and then Paula continued. "You know yesterday, when you finally came back, I found myself getting turned on to you."

"What was it that turned you on?"

"It was the whole package."

"No, seriously, I can't even find anything to like about myself lately. Name one thing!" said Ralph. "I am aging, I have a big mouth, and I am not spiritually or sexually enlightened!"

"I like your feet."

"My feet?"

"Yes, how your size fourteens fit in your big loafers. They are long and bony. I kind of like that. I got turned on! Go figure." They sat there bumper to bumper in traffic, quietly appreciating their animal closeness, smiling and musing.

"You know I'd miss you if you really disappeared or even died," she said.

"What kind of funeral would you give me?"

"How should I know? What would you like?"

"I believe that the planet is so populated already that I don't want to be just another body in a box in a cemetery. I'd want to be cremated. I hope you'll remember that." He paused before he spoke again. "*Can* you remember that? It is important! You really don't pay much attention to my requests!"

"Let's *see*. I think I should write it down to be sure. Why wouldn't I remember?"

"Because I've told you things like these before, and there are so many of my preferences that you conveniently forget. You arrive home with pumpernickel bagels when I asked you a million times for poppy seed. You know, those kinds of things."

"I'll remember. Will you remember when I die, that I want to be cremated too? I want a bench with a little bronze plaque with my name. The bench should overlook the water in Tiburon where you can sit and think after my memorial service is over. At my memorial service, I want you to play Nina Simone's rendition of 'I Did It My Way.'"

"What about food?"

"For food I want you to serve delicatessen from Max's. I want light on the mustard with really lean corned beef. As my friends leave, please blare Aretha Franklin's 'Freeway of Love.' I want a real send-off. How about you?"

Ralph started to hum the first line of "Freeway of Love" to get a rise out of her. Then he put his arm around her and pulled her close. She was straddling the bucket seats in the white Mustang like a teenage girl.

Ralph said, "I want vegetarian pizza from D'Angelo's at my blast-off. You know that they just started catering? Play Stravinsky's 'Firebird' and don't forget Mahler's Fourth. I want a bench, too. Do you think Marin County will be littered with benches from all the baby boomers and the 'It's-all-about-me generation,' by that time?"

"You know we could have had a real vacation?"

"You mean that this wasn't a real vacation?"

"Well, we could have gone to Italy or a remote island in Indonesia."

"Yeah, we could have had a real vacation where we could have struggled with the language. We could have gotten lost, exchanged dollars for sheckels. We could have gotten cheated, eaten weird food and come down with food poisoning. We could have lain in bed for days with dysentery and missed our plane, a real vacation!" shouted Ralph over the din of honking car horns.

"But at least we could have come back, and had jet lag for weeks and stories to tell our friends."

"I guess we couldn't share these stories, could we?"

"Tell our friends about our search for the G spot, are you crazy?"

"Couldn't we call it something else?"

"Like what?"

"How about the search for the G spot — as in Gratitude. I am so grateful that you are still in my life after all this. And we still love each other after all these years."

Ralph loved her at this moment, the very Paula who was manipulative, tough-edged, and filled with flaws, but then again, he recognized that so was he. He knew that she was his life partner, that despite all that they had put each other through the last several days, they had a history, and they fit together like Hansel and Gretel. They had gone through life together helping each other. They had been each other's teachers in sharing what life had to offer and its difficult challenges. Something had happened in these last few days and he knew that he would never abandon her because they had become deeply bonded by this experience.

"Oh, honey," was all Paula could say as she nuzzled closer to his reaching hand. She reached in her bag as they were nearing the airport and felt the bottle of anti-depressants that had been sitting there in the bottom of her purse. She had forgotten about those pills that Dr. Jacobs had given her. She took out one, blue with a smiling face, and pushed it back in the bottle under the protective cotton. She discreetly pressed the bottle under the passenger seat. Maybe the next occupant of the rental car would need these to cope with vacationing in paradise.

Acknowledgments

Stories are formed over time. With this in mind I have many people to thank for their support and inspiration:

Sharon Anderson, Linda Aroyan, Arlene Bernstein, Barbara and Larry Brauer, Susan Campbell, Elliott Chernin, Candace Fuhrman, Elsa Hurley, Gloria Kaiser, Erica Ross Kreiger, Gail Kossowsky, Annie Styron Leonard, George Leonard, Miriam Licht, Toni Littlejohn, Kate Lynch, Cyra McFadden, Jean McMann and the Writing Group, Gilda Meyers, Bryna Millman, Michael Murphy, Rod Napier, Sharon Norman, Karina and Stuart Oberman, Jean Parr, Nixy Rickles, Alison Ruedy, Fu Schroeder, the Friday morning meditation group, Catherine Stern and Abby Wasserman.